Aidan McQuade is a writer and independent human rights consultant. He comes from South Armagh in the North of Ireland.

Aidan was Director of Anti-Slavery International from 2006 to 2017. Prior to that, he worked extensively in development and humanitarian operations, including from 1996 to 2001 leading Oxfam GB's response to the brutal civil war in Angola.

He is the author of a professional book, *Ethical Leadership: Moral Decision Making Under Pressure*, and another novel, *The Undiscovered Country*.

In loving memory of our Siobhán

Aidan McQuade

SOME SERVICE TO THE STATE

AUSTIN MACAULEY PUBLISHERS™

LONDON • CAMBRIDGE • NEW YORK • SHARJAH

A CIP catalogue record for this title is available from the British Library.

ISBN 9781035817931 (Paperback)
ISBN 9781035817955 (ePub e-book)
ISBN 9781035817948 (Audiobook)

www.austinmacauley.com

First Published 2023
Austin Macauley Publishers Ltd®
1 Canada Square
Canary Wharf
London
E14 5AA

My first thanks go to my friends: Meena Varma, Deirdre Mortell, Karin de Jonge, Jill Heine, Tara Reynor O'Grady, Martin Hubbard, Joost Lina, Sophie Kramer, and, in particular my first reader, Eric "The Code" Hanby, who took upon themselves the thankless task of reading early drafts of this novel and provided me with the candid feedback essential to enable me to look at the text with fresh eyes, and to think new thoughts about the story when I felt that my brain was completely wrung dry.

My thanks also to Peter McEvoy and Eamon Hanna for sharing their reflections on the historical events that this book touches upon, particularly the Civil War and its aftermath. Peter, as well as providing feedback on an early draft, was an invaluable oral history source, sharing with me reminiscences and insights that he had gathered over the years directly from veterans of the 4th Northern Division of the old Irish Republican Army.

Finally, as always, my deepest thanks go to my beloved Klara Skrivankova, for putting up with my writing and all the absentmindedness and messiness it entails. It is she who suffers most for my art.

I would like to acknowledge 'Faber and Faber Ltd', for granting permission for publishing.

O land of password, handgrip, wink and nod,
Of open minds as open as a trap,
Where tongues lie coiled, as under flames lie wicks,
Where half of us, as in a wooden horse
Were cabin'd and confined like wily Greeks,
Besieged within the siege, whispering morse.

—Seamus Heaney, *Whatever you say, say nothing*

Part One: Mick

Newry, Northern Ireland

Saturday, 9 May 1925

I

"So, what are you saying? You want me to be your 'muscle'?"

"It's what you do, isn't it?" she said.

We were sitting in the café of the Shelbourne hotel in the middle of Newry, with coffee and cake that I could ill afford sitting between us. I really did not like the way this conversation was going.

"I mean, that was the essence of your duties as Republican Police, wasn't it?" she continued. "I would have thought that your time in a flying column would have honed your skills, made you a bit less squeamish about it." She always was a blunt one.

"Prison diminished the muscle though."

"You're looking well now though, Mick."

She is mocking me, I thought. The police had been rough enough when they arrested me, and during the interrogation in addition to general bruising and a couple of cracked ribs they had broken my nose and knocked out two of my molars. So I wasn't exactly threatening Valentino in the matinee idol stakes.

Still, I was grateful to the peelers that they had not simply carted me to the nearest ditch and put a bullet in my head. I still wasn't sure why I'd got so lucky that night. Maybe it was my Ma begging them for mercy, but I would have thought they would have been used to that sort of thing.

"I can't complain," I said. "Sure who would listen to me."

"How long have you been out now?"

"A couple of months."

"What was it like?"

Should I say it was like any other overcrowded rat-infested prison ship with overflowing toilets spilling shite into the dormitories? Maybe not.

"I've been better places. But at least I'm not dead yet."

She sipped her coffee and appraised me across the rim of her cup with those green eyes of hers. We must have seemed an incongruous pair, Sophia with her flame-red hair neatly coifed, manicured nails and elegant clothes, and me looking like a tramp she had taken pity on in the street. I was wearing an ill-fitting hand-me-down jacket from my brother, Joe, the cuffs of it and my shirt frayed, and my trousers were close to worn through at the knees.

"Look," she said. "I have had a patient that I am very worried about. She missed an appointment about a week ago and when I went to visit her at her home her father refused to let me see her. I asked my partners about it and they told me not to worry, that her medical attention is her parents' problem. But I am worried. She was very distressed when she came to see me, and it just doesn't feel right to me."

"I appreciate your concern, but I'm not sure what I can do about it."

"For God's sake, Mick. You're a local, near enough and I'm not. So you will automatically be treated with less suspicion than a blow-in like me. You're a man. You look scary. You were in the Republican Police, and I recall you have some experience making enquiries regarding the well-being of children. And you were in an IRA flying column. That should be enough to put the fear of God into anyone. Make them take us both a bit more seriously. At the moment I am getting fobbed off with horseshite at every turn."

I drank some coffee. "Scary?"

"That's a good thing. You've got that whole wild Irish thing going for you." She smiled. Cheeky bitch, I thought.

"I could pay you a few bob, Mick," she said.

"I have a job."

"What are you working at?"

"The abattoir."

"Given up dreams of becoming a barrister?"

"That idea faded somewhat in prison."

"What possessed you to go work in an abattoir though?"

"There's not much work about for anyone let alone an ex-jailbird. One can't get picky."

"I remember you throwing up when you attended a post-mortem I conducted."

"Aye. But I've gotten somewhat more used to killing since then."

She was quiet for a bit. "Still, I'm sure you could always use a bit more, buy the odd book?"

"There's a public library in town."

"Well, the occasional pint then?"

I looked at her, her eyes glittering at me across the table like the last time I saw her in the kitchen of her home in Mayo.

15

Though it was only a couple of years it seemed a lifetime ago. It was before the flying column. Before I had killed anyone. Before prison.

Sitting before her now I became aware of her perfume, probably French, I thought, filling my head.

Fuck it, I thought to myself. Do I have anything better to do on a Saturday?

"So what else can you tell me about this girl?" I asked.

"You understand Mick that what I tell you has to be in the strictest confidence? I am breaching a patient's confidentiality here, but I feel I am ethically justified given my concerns about her well-being."

"I understand," I said. "Go on."

"Her family come from around Jonesborough."

"Neighbours almost. What is her name?"

"Hoey. Collette Hoey. Do you know her?"

"No. But I think I have heard tell of the Hoeys. It's a common enough name around South Armagh, I suppose. What's her Da's name?"

"Cathal. Does that help?"

Had I heard that name somewhere? In jail, maybe? "It rings a vague bell. Anything else?"

"She's pregnant."

"Of course she is," I said. "How far along?"

"She'd be just over two months by now."

"Do we know the happy daddy?"

"That's not really the important thing right now."

"It might be if they've run off to New York or Paris together to live happily ever after."

"She's fourteen. She shouldn't be running off anywhere."

"Fourteen? Jesus!" I said.

"I know."

"How long has she been your patient?"

"Not at all long. I have just met her the once."

"She made an impression then?"

"She did. She was a bright girl but she was very distressed. She knew she was pregnant soon after she missed her period. But she was hoping against hope that she wasn't."

"Why you? Were you the family doctor?"

"No. She said she sought me out because I was a woman. Understandably enough I don't think she felt she wanted to talk to a male doctor about her condition."

"So have you spoke to the Da?"

"Her Da or the baby's?"

"Both."

"Like I said, her Da told me to fuck off and mind my own business."

"What about her mother?"

"Her mother is dead."

"Dead long?"

"According to what Collette told me, since she was little, four or five years old. Around the time she first went to national school."

"What about the baby's Da?"

"She mentioned the name of a young fellow called McCreevy, from around the village over, Dromintee."

"What age of a fella?"

"Not sure. She said about sixteen."

"Do you know his first name?"

"Anthony."

"Do you know his address?"

"Yes. I did a bit of asking about."

"Have you spoken to him yet?"

"No."

"So as far as we know this young fellow could still be blissfully unaware that he is to be a father."

"I imagine that is a possibility."

"Did you ask in her school about her?"

"She was at Our Lady's in town. I spoke to the headmistress. She said her father had informed her she was taking her out of school and taking her to another, closer to her home."

"Closer to Jonesborough? Sure apart from Newry the closest secondary schools would be in Dundalk and that's hardly closer."

"I'm just telling you what she told me. But yes. It's horseshite."

"She didn't mention which school?"

"She said she didn't know, and would have regarded the information as privileged if she did."

"Privileged? Really? I never knew the name of your school would ever be thought of as confidential, particularly to the girl's doctor."

"I know. That's another thing that's been bothering me."

"Maybe they just didn't like the idea of giving the information out to a Protestant."

"Sure how would they know that?"

"Nuns can spot a Protestant at 200 yards."

"Is that just an assumption about personal hygiene?"

"That and eyes. Them Protestant eyes are a desperate give away," I said.

"I know I'm going to regret this," said Sophia, "but what exactly is the difference between Protestant and Catholic eyes?"

"Protestant eyes are closer together and generally squinty with disapproval."

"Hmm," she said, giving me a disapproving look with her perfectly spaced eyes.

I drained my coffee. Out of the corner of my eye I saw the waitress. "Excuse me," I said to her, "Can I have the bill please?"

"I've paid already," said Sophia.

"When did you do that?"

"When you were at the toilet. I thought you might try to be gallant, and didn't have time for that oul shite."

"Oh," I said. "That's very kind."

"It was me invited you."

"Still very kind."

"Not at all," and she took a forkful of the rich fruit cake she had on the plate before her. "Are you sure you don't want some of this. It's really nice." If truth be told my teeth were watering at the sight of it, but I hadn't ordered any for myself because I thought I was going to have to foot the bill.

"You know I wouldn't mind a taste."

She cut the cake in half with the edge of her fork and pushed it towards me. I scooped it up and swallowed it in one mouthful. For a moment I was back in prison at the Christmas just passed, when Frank Campbell had shared out amongst us a cake he'd received from his family.

Sophia's voice brought me back to the present. "So, what next then?"

"I suppose we could have another word with her Da," I said. "See if he'll be a bit more forthcoming man to man. Do you still have that shiny automobile of yours?" I asked.

"I do."

"Grand so. I don't fancy cycling around the countryside balancing you on my crossbar."

I stood up.

"So we're off then?"

"Aye. No time to waste. I've a hectic social whirl planned for this evening."

"But I haven't finished my coffee."

"Sorry," I said and I sat back down and watched her as she raised her cup to her lips. She took a long sip. "This place does make nice coffee. I love Mayo, but decent coffee was sometimes hard to get."

"Particularly with the likes of me disrupting trains and transport for months on end."

"Those were certainly the most difficult days." She lifted her cup again and took a final swallow. "Ready now," she said as she set the cup down and stood up.

I hauled myself back to my feet. As I did I noticed that her lipstick had marked the rim of the white china that she had been drinking from.

It was like a smear of bright blood.

II

I had received a letter from Sophia earlier that week. It was a bit of a surprise as I had not seen or heard from her since 1920. Not that I ever expected to. Our acquaintance had been brief.

The letter was quite formal. She wrote that she had moved to Newry the previous year to join as a partner in an established medical practice and that she would appreciate a conversation regarding a professional problem that she was trying to deal with. She suggested the time and place if I was able to meet.

I was curious what she wanted. When I had known her in Mayo I was working with the Republican Police, a formation she had described, perhaps with a modicum of justice, as 'Keystone Cops'. Beyond that I didn't suppose I had left much of an impression on her from the short time I had known her, before I had joined a flying column and spent the next eight months tramping and fighting across bleak stretches of the west of Ireland.

At least, I thought, I might get a decent cup of coffee out of the meeting. So I sent her a note to the return address—her medical practice—confirming that I would see her the next Saturday morning.

In spite of my low expectations I still found myself surprisingly disappointed that she seemed to remember me primarily as a glorified thug. After all, I had read a few books and I even almost had a law degree once. But I consoled myself: it is better to leave a bad impression than none at all. And, to be fair, when I reflected on it, a glorified thug is what I had been, albeit in what I thought was a good cause. However, finding myself now on the wrong side of the border following Partition, there was not much of the glorification. Instead I was a subject of suspicion and some degree of hatred to the British and Unionist authorities who were still entrenched north of the border. I was that most dreadful of things to them: a Paddy who did not seem to know his proper place in the imperial order.

We picked up her car from Sophia's home and drove out of town up the Dublin Road and then took a right at the new church at Cloughoge and headed up the Forkhill Road.

"It's more direct up the Dublin Road," I said.

"I know," she said, "but this way we can avoid the border posts."

"When did you last visit?" I asked.

"Last week. Just before I wrote to you."

"How did you get my address?"

"You do know you're a figure of some notoriety in these parts, don't you? I asked around. One of our receptionists knows your people."

"Jesus. You could have taught Mick Collins a thing or two about intelligence gathering."

"He seemed to do rightly on his own."

We drove on, towards Meigh where Sophia took a left off the Forkhill Road and traced her way through a maze of side roads which she seemed to know as well as any local.

"You know where you're going?"

"I think I remember it."

I had not been out this way since I got out of prison. That meant I had not been this way since the British imposed their meandering border here. But as the car brushed the outskirts of Jonesborough it dawned on me that Sophia's patient was, in fact, a resident of the newly formed Irish Free State, rather than Northern Ireland.

"You have many patients from the Free State?" I asked.

"A few," she said. "Sure they're closer to Newry than Dundalk here."

We turned a bend in the road. "There it is," said Sophia.

We pulled up outside the gate of the house. Sophia switched off the engine and I unfolded myself out of the car and took a look at the house. It was a substantial affair, white-washed with red trim and a black slate roof. The front of the house was a rose garden while the back was the farm outhouses, byres and barns.

Sophia joined me from the other side of the car. "Not too shabby," I said.

"It's not," said Sophia. "Shall we?"

"Aye," I said. "No point fucking about."

I opened that gate and followed Sophia through it and up the footpath to the front door. An iron bell-pull hung to the side of the porch. I pulled it and we heard the bell sound deep in the house. We looked at each other.

"Are you going to do the talking?" I asked.

"Let's play it by ear," she said.

There was a sound of movement from within the house and then that of a bolt being drawn on the scarlet door before us. It creaked open and a young girl of about ten or eleven stood there, wrapped in an apron.

"We are here to see Mr Hoey?" Sophia said.

"He's out the byre," said the girl. "What is it about?"

"Could you tell him Dr Hennessy is here to see him again please?"

She turned to go, not closing the door, but not exactly welcoming us in either. I put my hand to it and widened it open. She turned at the creaking of the heavy door. "Maybe we could wait inside?" I asked. She hesitated and then said, "Come in here please."

We followed her down the hall a short way and she opened the door of a parlour to us. "Wait here please and I'll go and get my Da."

"Just a minute," said Sophia. The girl hesitated on the threshold of the room.

"What's your name?" Sophia asked.

"Mairead."

"That's a nice name. What school are you at, Mairead?"

"I was at Jonesborough this year, but I'm going to St Louis's in September."

"In Dundalk."

"Yes."

"That's exciting. You must be very smart to be going there."

The girl smiled.

"Listen," said Sophia, "We really came to see your sister, Collette. Is she here?"

The girl's smile melted away. "I'll get my Da," she said, and before anyone could say anything more she fled.

We entered the parlour, a bright clean room, sparsely decorated but with a large three piece leather suite set before an empty fire grate. I slumped myself into an armchair while Sophia made a circumnavigation of the room, stopping by the bay windows to look out on the garden.

"So how are you finding Newry?" I asked, by way of making conversation as we waited.

"It's not too bad," she said.

"The Belfast Road is a nice part of town. Neat and tidy with all them Protestants."

"Well, I would like to be more ecumenical Mick, but it is cleaner out that way, do you not think?"

"It is," I said. "That is certainly something I have always admired about your culture. It's attention to cleanliness. I've heard it's next to Godliness. I've sometimes thought that the Protestants of these parts like it even more than tray bakes."

"I'm not sure I'd go that far, Mick, but they keep tolerable standards."

We heard the clump of heavy boots coming up the hallway. I jumped out of the chair. I had the sudden thought that if he was anything like my Da he could be possessive about where he sat, and there was no point in antagonising him from the outset by being caught in his favourite armchair.

The door swung open with a creak and a hulking man who I presumed was Hoey stood in the doorway. He spoke before either Sophia or I could say a thing. "I thought I told you that you were not welcome here?" he said. So, I needn't have worried: he was antagonised from the off anyway.

He was a man who looked in his middle thirties. Lean and powerfully built, about my height but heavier set and, given his vigorous air and ruddy complexion, someone who was used to the outdoor life.

"I'm sorry Mr Hoey, but as I told you last week, I have some serious health concerns about Collette."

"Well, that's none of your concern now. She has new medical care and they will be seeing to her needs now."

"If that is the case they should have been in touch with me for her medical records, and no one has."

"I imagine they'll get around to that."

"Well, if you could tell me the name of her new doctor I would be happy to speak to them directly."

"I'm saying nothing to you but fuck off." He said that with a vehemence that made my hairs stand on end.

"There's no need for that sort of language now," I managed to stammer out. "The doctor is only concerned about your daughter. There's many would be grateful for this sort of attention."

He turned on me. "Who the fuck are you? Her fancy man?" I felt my face lightly splashed with his spittle.

"There's been nothing fancy about me in my entire life," I said.

"Mick is a colleague from my previous work," Sophia said. "I asked him to accompany me as he's local and knows his way about better than me. I'm always afraid of getting lost on the roads."

"Mick who?" he asked.

"Mick McAlinden," I said.

"Gerry McAlinden's son, from Killean?"

"Aye, that's me."

Hoey let out a snort and turned to Sophia. "Are you trying to intimidate me with the IRA?"

"What do you mean?" asked Sophia, playing innocent.

"I've heard of this blade. Big man with a flying column down South, doesn't know enough not to get lifted when he's back visiting his Ma."

There was a lot of that I couldn't disagree with. I had been dumb enough to think the Truce with the British would be the end of it. But, of course, it wasn't. Is it ever? I was still pondering what side I was going to take, if any, in the post-Treaty Civil War when the newly formed Royal Ulster Constabulary had kicked in the door of my parents' house and carted me off to prison. Perhaps they had done me two favours that night: not only had they not plugged me in the skull but they had ensured I did not have to make that choice in the end.

Certainly I had little stomach for picking up a gun against former comrades.

"Actually I was in a flying column in the West not the South," I said. I thought if I couldn't dispute the facts of his case I could at least be pedantic about the way he put it.

"Like I give a fuck. I was assistant quartermaster for the 4th Northern Division of the IRA. So," Hoey said turning to Sophia, "if you'd hoped to scare me with some washed up gunman you have come to the wrong place. More dangerous men than this gobshite have tried worse before now."

"I'm not trying to threaten anyone with anybody. All I'm trying to do is attend to a patient about whom I have concerns," said Sophia.

"What concerns? I'm her father. Tell me what concerns you have."

"There are certain confidences that are essential between a doctor and her patient?"

"She's fourteen. Any child of mine living under my roof shouldn't be keeping secrets from their father."

"Well, she doesn't appear to be living under your roof at the moment does she?" said Sophia.

Hoey's face flushed from deep pink to a light shade of purple at that. "Listen Miss Madam, I've asked you nicely to leave. I am very shortly going to be less polite."

"Jesus," I said. "If you think you've been polite your Ma must have dropped you on your head when you were a baby."

For a big man he moved fast and I barely saw the left hand he struck me with. He caught me just below my eye and with such force that I stumbled back, tripped myself up on the armchair and landed dazed on my backside against the wall and on the floor. I felt a blood vessel burst in my nose and the blood begin to flow. I tried to wipe some away with my hand.

"Jesus Christ," said Sophia.

Looking up I saw Hoey begin to move towards me again. I tried to push myself to my feet gaining just the tiniest of satisfactions that I was dripping blood on his carpet in the process. This is not going to be good I thought as he loomed over me.

Just then Sophia caught his left arm from behind and tried to restrain him. She was barely half his size, but she held on to him like a terrier that he could not shake off. That distracted him enough that he turned his attention from me and twisted back towards her with his right fist cocked. He had scruple enough, though, about hitting a woman, at least with a witness present, not to let fly.

"Get out, before I throw the two of you out of here on your arses."

I pushed myself back onto my feet. Discretion, I always thought, was the better part of valour. "Come on, Sophia," I said. She let go of his arm and moved between us. He lowered his fist slightly and we circled each other as we moved towards the door, all the time facing him, watching for any more sudden moves. I found the door handle behind me and opened it. "Come on Sophia," I said again.

"You first," she said.

"No you."

"I don't care which of you it is, just fuck off out of here and don't come back," said Hoey.

We backed out of the parlour, me first, Sophia after, still keeping herself between me and Hoey. We reversed back down the hallway, through the front door, and up the pathway to the gate. Neither of us turning our back on him until we had the gate between us and bolted again, though he could have jumped it if he had a mind to. He followed us each step of the way and then leaned on the gate as he watched us move towards the car.

"Ask around about me if you want McAlinden," he said, as I was about to get into the car, "and let your girlfriend know that I'm serious when I say this: come this way again sticking her nose into my business, and I'll happily put her and you and anyone else you care to bring into the ground."

Sophia was inside the car already and had started the engine. But she heard clearly Hoey's threat through her open window. "Get in Mick," she hissed, "for God's sake." But I hesitated and, still dripping blood, turned to look him in the eye. He looked back and straight through me. I had seen that look before, years ago in the West, and in prison amongst guards and prisoners alike. It was the look of a man accustomed to killing.

III

As soon as I closed the car door Sophia accelerated away from the house. She drove wordlessly and fast for about half a mile before pulling into the gateway of a field and switching off the engine.

"Fuck," she said.

"Aye."

She turned towards me. "Let me look at your face," she said and she reached into the back of the car to retrieve her medical bag.

"It's fine." I had pulled a relatively clean handkerchief out of my pocket and was concentrating on slowing the blood flow from my nose.

"I'll be the fucking judge of that," she shouted. But then it had been a stressful morning.

I turned my face to her as she opened her bag. She took out a clean cloth and gently wiped my nose and mouth and leaned in to look more closely. I felt her breath on my skin.

"Fortunately he didn't cut you so you won't be needing stitches, but I'm afraid you're going to have a black eye. Now hold this to your nose…" she placed my hand on the cloth, "…and lean your head back."

"Not forward?" I asked.

"Only if you're prepared to mop out the floor of my car afterwards."

I complied with her instructions and leaned back. I remembered she could be a fierce one when she was minded. And, after having had my arse scalped once this morning, I did not feel like a second helping.

"Shite," I said. "How am I going to explain this to my Ma."

"Really? That's what you're thinking about at the moment?"

"Irish mammies. They worry."

"You are remembering that that fucker threatened to kill us just now." I heard her striking a match and lighting herself a cigarette. I had given up smoking in jail but that smoke was delicious.

"I've dealt with fuckers like him before."

"Maybe when they were in the Black and Tans. But you're short a flying column here."

"Aye. It would probably have helped if I'd known he was in the IRA himself. Your intelligence network didn't mention that to you?"

"Fuck sake, you're the local here. Isn't that what I'm paying you for?"

"You're not fucking paying me. And anyway I thought you just wanted me to look scary. You didn't remember that we were dropping in on Finn Mc-Fucking-Cool. The last time that fucker was scared by anything was probably the age of the dinosaurs."

That made her laugh for a second.

Then she went quiet as she appraised the mess that was my face. I inspected the cloth briefly. I was still bleeding so I put it back.

"Thanks for stopping him doing more damage. I was in real trouble when I went down there."

"I thought you were a man accustomed to violence, Mick. How did he catch you so off-guard."

"I really wasn't expecting this when I got up this morning. And I've gotten a bit out of practice. Unless you're talking about cattle. But they tend not to have dangerous left hands."

She let out a giggle at that too. "I'm sorry Mick. I didn't think this would happen. I just thought he might be just a bit more cooperative if there was a man present."

"Well, it should please your suffragette heart to learn then that it appears he's not got anything in particular against women. He's just a prick to everyone."

"It's not the most comforting news I've ever received."

"Do you think he knows?"

"What?"

"That Collette is pregnant. He wouldn't be showing that level of testiness if you were worrying about an in-growing toenail."

"I don't know," said Sophia.

"Maybe she confided in him."

"Maybe she did. That is a level of crankiness that I've seen before."

"Where did you see it?"

"My own father. When I brought my husband Charlie home to meet him for the first time. He spent the whole of dinner fuming. I think he realised that we were already lovers. Fathers can be very proprietorial about their daughters' sexuality. All that notion of bringing shame on the household."

I pondered for a minute on this. "Jesus," I said, "you had a much more interesting university career than me."

"Dublin," she said.

"Aye."

We sat for a while in silence as I concentrated on stopping bleeding. After a while I looked at the cloth again. I seemed to have stopped so I sat forward.

"Look," I said, "isn't this over and above what is expected of you already? Her father tells us she's fine. Can't we leave it at that?"

"I'd still like to know where she is."

"I was afraid you'd say that. Why? What's bothering you?"

"Well, I've been a doctor a while now, and that is actually the first time that I've been threatened with murder for enquiring after the health of a patient."

I was quiet for a while. Sophia had heard what Hoey had said, but she hadn't seen the look in his eyes. "I don't think that threat was just bravado. I've met his sort before." I felt a cold sweat breaking on my forehead at the thought of it.

"Exactly. The sort of murderous bastard that has been afflicting the women of Ireland for centuries."

"We're hardly going to rectify that whole system of injustice in one Saturday afternoon."

"One thing at a time, Mick. Let's just see if we can find out if Collette is safe and well."

"Hmm," I said.

"So any ideas?"

"What about?"

"About finding Collette Hoey."

"Fuck," I said. I was still preoccupied by that look in Hoey's eyes and the thought of what he might have done to me if Sophia hadn't got between us. Sophia was right. Hoey was a bully and I doubted that he would have scruple to refrain from bullying women and girls in the privacy of his own home. I did fucking hate bullies. I hated them in principle, and I hated this one in particular. There would be some considerable satisfaction in fucking that fucker over.

Sophia was staring at me with some intensity. "Okay," I said. "Let's go and see young Don Juan McCreevy and see if he knows anything. I mean if I can't intimidate a sixteen year old there really is no more hope for me."

IV

The shortest road to Dromintee would have taken us back past Hoey's front door. So I suggested instead that we take a bit of a diversion back up to the Forkhill Road and approach it from that direction, past the craggy face of Slieve Gullion.

Sophia had written the address of the McCreevy's on a piece of paper, but we still had to ask directions a couple of times to track down the right house on the right road.

We pulled up on the roadside just before the entrance to the McCreevy farm. It was a more modest affair than that of the Hoey's, but it was still a well-attended, single storey cottage with wildflowers growing in front and an assortment of sheds at the back.

"Right so," I said and opened the car door.

"Hold on, Mick. What are we going to say?"

"Well, I was going to open with, 'Hello Anthony'."

"But what if he's not there? Or somebody else answers the door? Are we going to tell his mother that we want to chat to him about his approaching fatherhood?"

"Hmm," I said. "Don't you have any legitimate doctor things you could talk to him about?"

"Well, I might if he was my patient, but he's not."

"Couldn't you just tell him you think he might have the clap?"

"Jesus, Mick. The young fella is sixteen years old. Even if that was even marginally ethical, I'm not going to mentally torture a youngster who has done nothing wrong."

"Wages of sin though?"

"Enough of that oul shite."

"Jesus, you're a disappointing Protestant. Not only no evidence of sectarianism but not so much on the rush to judgement front either. Do you have any hobbies at all?"

"Traybakes! Like all good Protestants."

I laughed at that. "So how were you planning on going about this?" I asked.

"I wasn't planning at all. I thought you had this already worked out what with all that investigative experience you have going for you."

I closed the door again and turned to look at her. "Sarcasm is the lowest form of wit," I said.

"Aye. But it's the highest form of intelligence." I'd never noticed her saying "aye" before. Maybe she was going native.

"So, let's have some of that highest form of intelligence then. What are we going to do?"

"I suppose we'll have to wait," she said.

Sophia took a look about her and then eased the car back into gear and drove up the road about a hundred yards to where a gate opened beneath a sycamore tree. There she manoeuvred the car until it was facing back towards the McCreevy home. She switched off the engine and we both stared down the road towards the cottage.

"So what do you know about young McCreevy?" I asked.

"Well, he sounds like a bright fella. He's at St Colman's College in Newry and he plays football."

"Aye, that's what all the girls want. A local hero on the football pitch."

"Did you play football at school?"

"I couldn't kick snow off a ditch."

"Hence all that romantic disappointment and bitterness."

"Exactly," I said.

"It's good that you're so in touch with your emotions, Mick."

"I'd much time to reflect in jail."

"Any other useful skills you developed when you were inside?"

"I suppose I should have been more assiduous at the French and Irish classes, but mostly I just read when I could. I did give up smoking though."

"Why?" Sophia asked.

"It was such a palaver to get tobacco, it seemed simpler just to give it up. No matter what anyone else says, it always seemed a bad idea to me to be inhaling all that soot."

"Why did you ever start then?"

"I found my IRA duties stressful. Cigarettes were a bit of a relief."

We fell silent for a while and watched. I was still inclined to go and knock at the door, like a normal person. But Sophia was right. This wasn't exactly a normal visit.

After a while a woman emerged from the back of the house carrying a basket on her hip. She was probably in her middle thirties, but she looked older. She walked with a slight stoop and I could make out wisps of grey in her hair. Her bearing suggested that life hadn't been the kindest to her. She disappeared behind a barn and we waited on. After about five minutes she came into view again, this time the basket looked filled with dried washing and she disappeared back into the house.

"I think I should probably speak to the young fella by myself?" I said.

"Why so?"

"Well, whatever his romantic exploits, you're right. He's still only a youngster. He might be too embarrassed and tongue-tied to speak to a woman."

"I don't want you bullying him."

36

"You're on a bit of a fine line there, Sophia. You specifically said you wanted me because I looked a bit scary. And if I learned one thing in the Republican Police, a bit of fear is sometimes your only advantage."

"Hmm," said Sophia. "You might be right. So what will you ask him?"

"I think I'll start with when did he last see Collette and I'll work up to when did he start skewering her."

"I presume you will paraphrase that last question."

"Probably," I said.

We waited about another half an hour. Eventually a young man appeared from around the corner of his house. He was wheeling a bicycle and had a satchel on his back.

"Is that him?" I asked.

"Could be," Sophia said.

"Let's see then." I opened the car door and jumped out.

I quicken my pace towards the McCreevy's yard gate and got there just as the boy was bolting it behind him.

"Anthony?" I asked.

He looked up and caught his breath at the sight of me.

"Sorry," I said. "I walked into a door this morning."

He was a good-looking young lad with dark hair and eyes and an athletic frame. But there was a shyness about him when he answered.

"I am. Who are you?"

I extended my hand to him. As he took it I said, "My name's Mick McAlinden. I come from over Killean way."

He tentatively reached out to me and uncertainly shook my hand. "What brings you here?" he asked.

"I was hoping for a quick word with you Anthony, if you don't mind."

"With me?"

"Aye."

"What about?"

"Collette Hoey."

He blinked. "What about her?" he asked.

"I understand you're friendly with her."

"A bit."

"When was the last time you saw her?"

"About two weeks ago, I suppose."

"Not since then?"

"No."

"Why not?"

"Why should I?"

"I heard you were doing a line with her?"

"Who told you that?"

"It doesn't matter who told me. Were you?"

"I wasn't."

"So why are people telling me that you were?"

"I've no idea. What's it to you anyway?"

I thought I'd probably better tell him something of the truth. It might break him in gently to the paternal changes the appeared to loom in his life.

"Collette's not shown up to her doctor's appointments. Her doctor is worried about her so she asked me to see if I could find out what had happened to her?"

"Are you a peeler?"

"No. I used to be Republican Police though, down in Mayo. Before I joined a flying column."

I'm not proud of it. But even the short time I had been out of jail I had discovered that in certain circumstances throwing in a bit of IRA into a conversation could gain you a degree of respect that you would never normally earn from just your looks, brains or personality.

"Oh," Anthony said, and he swallowed.

"So, what was the craic with you and Collette?" I asked.

"I saw her at a couple of dances and ceilidhs. Spoke to her after Mass, would bump into her in the library in town some weekends. That's about it?"

"Really?"

"Really," he said.

"What did you talk to her about?"

"Books and school stuff mostly. Last time I spoke to her she was telling me she was having difficulties with her French. I told her to stick with it, that it got better with practice. And she had just started reading Shakespeare."

"Which one?"

"*Two Gentlemen of Verona*, I think. She was finding that difficult too."

"I've not read that one. Is that the one with the dog or the bear?"

"The dog. The bear is in *The Winter's Tale*."

"Did she ever talk about anything else?"

"What like?"

"About home life? About her plans for the future?"

"She might have. But why should I tell you anything about that?"

I don't know if I'd been expecting him to tell me of a shared love of philosophy or poetry, perhaps to describe two special souls—scholarship kids both, after all—finding each other in the mists and rains of South Armagh. But, of course, they were just kids. So much of life was about school. But, I thought, so much of the rest was about hormones.

I looked at him. He looked at his feet. For a minute neither of us said anything.

Finally, when I decided he'd suffered enough, I said, "I'd heard there was more to it than that."

"What did you hear?"

"I heard it was pretty serious between the two of you."

"Who told you that?"

"What are you worried about Anthony? Collette was a good looking girl. You were doing well to go out with the likes of her."

"Well, we weren't going out."

"Not ever?"

"No, not ever." He shuffled again, avoiding my eyes, looking at his feet. Then, "Look, I've got a match to get to, so I need to be off."

"Sure, no worries. I can walk with you a bit."

Anthony blanched and didn't move. "Look, mister. There isn't anything that I can tell you. I saw her a couple of times at a couple of dances. I had a couple of dances with her. I didn't fancy her. I just danced with her cos I felt sorry for her. She seemed a bit shy, a bit lonely. And she seemed to want to talk to me about school and stuff every so often. I was a year or so ahead so she thought I might be able to help her with some stuff."

"Some stuff?"

"Yes."

"So not just school?"

"Do I look like some sort of gossiping schoolgirl to you?" Anthony asked.

"You don't."

"So IRA or not, I'm not going to tell you anything I was told in confidence."

"That sounds very chivalrous. You're a gentleman so."

"My parents taught me right from wrong."

In that moment I felt so sorry for Anthony. In spite of his words of defiance, he had a forlorn look about him and his story had a right of truth to it. But, I'd been interrogated a couple of times myself. Rule number one: don't talk. Of course, you talk if you're scared, and I'd been scared myself more than once over the past few years. So rule number two: if you are going to talk try to stick close to the truth. Just try to leave out the interesting bits, like where the guns are buried, or the bodies.

But that was not my job today. Today, my job was to find out where Collette was.

"Here's the thing though, Anthony. I know how grateful young girls can be to their knights in shining armour. Sure no one would judge you if things went a bit further than a dance."

He looked at me straight at that, a look of shock on his face.

"Fuck," he said, as if just realising what I had been dancing around since we started talking.

"That's one way of putting it."

"If anyone says that about me," said Anthony, "they're a fucking liar."

"Anthony," I said. But he had become animated with something akin to anger, or embarrassment, and he turned from me and threw his leg over his bicycle and started off.

"No worries, Anthony," I said. "I'll just have a word with your Ma."

He slammed on the brakes of his bike and pivoted back round towards me. He did not come closer though. That suggested that in spite of his anger he was still a bit wary of me, I thought.

"You go and talk to my Ma if you like. She'll tell you what I've just told you. And if you don't believe her, you can speak to my Da too. And I can give you the names and addresses of all my uncles and aunts if you want to speak to them. And they'll tell you the same thing. And then they'll tell you that you can fuck off back to Killean to whatever mangy sheep will have you and leave us in peace."

With that he steered his bicycle back around and sped off, presumably in the direction of whatever football pitch his match was at. I watched him go.

Years later I learned an American word: chutzpah. At the time I just thought, "Fair play to you Anthony. You've got balls."

V

I heard the car engine starting up behind me and turned to see Sophia manoeuvring the vehicle slowly towards me. I waited until she came alongside and then walked behind the car and got into the passenger side. She switched off her engine.

"So," she asked. "What's the story?"

"Just drive away from the house a bit, would you. I don't want his Ma chasing us with a wooden spoon."

Sophia started the engine again, put the car into gear, and drove up the road a bit until she found another place where she could pull into the side of the road. She switched off the engine, pulled on the handbrake, and then reaching over to the glove compartment in front of me, took out a cigarette case and box of matches. She sparked up, breathed deeply and then exhaled a cloud of blue smoke.

"So," she asked again. "What's the craic?"

I eased open the window. "He denies everything."

"What? He claims he didn't know her?"

"No. He says he knew her. But denies that he did anything more than dance with her a few times because he felt sorry for her, and had a chat or two about school after Mass."

"Did you believe him?"

"Maybe. But some folk have a talent for lying."

"Do you think he is one such?"

"Hmm," I said. I was quiet for a minute going back over our conversation.

"Here's the thing," I said. "He told me to go and ask his Ma if I didn't believe him."

"What? Irish mothers always believe their sons are above reproach. She'd hardly be an impartial witness."

"I know. But I'm not talking about a court of law. I don't think most Irish males are into discussions of their romantic adventures with their mothers. I mean I'm pretty sure that at that age in particular they are not keen to involve their mothers in anything with even the hint of shenanigans."

"So?"

"So, he was pretty sharp in telling me I could talk to his ma for all he cared when I threatened it. Suggests to me that there's nothing there. If there was something there, he'd have bricked it."

"Hmm," said Sophia.

"He also hinted that Collette and he had discussed more than schoolwork."

"Did he tell you what?"

"No. He was pretty clear he would not be betraying confidences."

"He said that?" Sophia asked.

"I think his actual words were an imaginative variation of, 'Why don't you go and fuck yourself,' but that's what he meant."

"He what?"

"Seems like I can't even intimidate a sixteen year old kid anymore."

"Did he know you were IRA?"

"He did. But there is a lot of IRA about here. You know what they say about familiarity."

"So, where does that leave us?" she asked.

I closed my eyes for another minute to think. "I'm afraid I think that this trail is cold. It may be an idea to approach the other schools round about to ask after her. Dundalk would be the best place to start," I said. "Beyond that, for the moment at least, I'm out of notions."

"Well," she said, "I don't suppose there is much use asking you to do that."

"No," I said. "Adult male, not the father, asking after young girl. Likely to draw attention of the authorities, if you're lucky."

"What if you're unlucky?"

"A bit unlucky and I'd likely be facing Collette's Da's shotgun. Really unlucky and I have wooden ruler armed nuns beating me about the head again."

She took another drag on her cigarette and exhaled. "I have a day off this Wednesday," she said. "Maybe I can drive up to Dundalk and ask a few questions."

"That would seem to be a reasonable next step if you want to keep at this."

"I do."

"Okay then. If I have any other bright ideas I'll drop a note into your surgery. But otherwise I think we are done for today. Will you drop me back to my bicycle?"

"Maybe I could buy you an early dinner first? This day, I think, has been rather more than you bargained for. It's the least I can do."

At the mention of food I felt the hunger rising in me. "Thanks," I said. "That would be very nice."

"Grand so," she said, and took a final drag on her cigarette, threw it out of the window, and started the car. "Shall we go to Carlingford? I could do with a bit of sea air."

"Sure, why not?" I said, and she put the car into gear.

VI

There was a pleasant breeze coming off the water as we sat down at an outside table. Across Carlingford Lough the Mournes swept up from the sea in the spring sunshine. "Sure you wouldn't get a view like this in Paris," Sophia said.

I had a pint with me, but Sophia was confining herself to a lemonade as we awaited our lunch being brought to us. I had intended just to have a sandwich but Sophia had convinced me to have the oysters instead. "The Carlingford oysters are really good," she assured me.

"I've never eaten an oyster in my life."

"Time to start then. You don't want to go through life missing all of the good things."

When the oysters arrived I was taken aback by the look of them. They lay on their half shells, the colour of wet iron and I was instinctively repulsed at their rawness. I had read enough to know that they were not meant to be cooked. Still, they were not the most appetising thing I had ever seen.

However, I didn't want to appear a complete Philistine in front of Sophia so I listened as she instructed me how to eat them. "Squeeze a bit of lemon juice on them. That stuns them, makes their final moments going down your throat a bit more bearable," she told me solemnly. I'm still not sure if she was joking.

I swallowed the first one down. I am not sure what I was expecting, but their cool, silken texture and the tang of the sea surprised me.

"Verdict?" Sophia asked.

"You know, I'm not sure," I said. "It's not really a ham bap."

"It's not. Maybe they are more of an acquired taste."

"Why would anyone want to acquire it."

"I've heard tell they are an aphrodisiac."

"Really?"

"'Tis said. The Romans used to pack them in hay and snow and cart them over the Alps into Italy to feed their appetites."

"That sounds right: a bunch of dirty bastards the lot of them."

"You've studied them?"

"Bits and pieces," I said. "I did Latin at school, so I've read parts of the *Aeneid* and the *Gallic Wars*. When I was in jail I read a lump of Gibbon's *Decline and Fall*."

"Isn't that the one that blames Catholics for everything?"

"He has a dig at all Christians. But he was English so I suspect he was particularly pissed off with the Catholics."

"He'd been tempted to become a Catholic when he was young, you know. So he probably wanted to reassure the Establishment that he was back on side after that youthful wobble," she said.

"No better way of reassuring them than enthusiastically sticking the boot into those who were once your friends or own community."

"You suffer," she said.

"'Tis true. But it's not just the Irish or the Catholics, is it? It's what Josephus did when he betrayed his own people to the Romans. It's what Kit Carson did when he betrayed his Navajo friends and family to the United States."

"It's what happened to the French Protestants on St Bartholemew's day too. I imagine that there are still Protestant minorities in some parts of the world experiencing similar things."

"Aye. It's the lesson of the schoolyard isn't it. People gang up. They love the feeling they get when they can visit misery on someone weaker."

"It is," said Sophia. "But at least kids have the excuse of being kids. Adults have no such excuse. And yet in proper supposed democracies, majorities give minorities dog's abuse when they have the chance."

"I suppose that makes it understandable why some jump the fence if they can, even if it is still contemptable," I said.

I took a slug of my porter and then swallowed down another oyster. After the surprise of the first one, I began to see what Sophia was saying about people acquiring a taste for them.

"So, what are your plans, Mick?"

"What do you mean?"

"I mean you aren't planning on working in an abattoir all your life are you?"

"It's a job."

"Not one for a man who has read Virgil and Caesar."

"You'd be surprised."

"Be serious now."

"I don't know how things look in your part of town, Sophia, but from where I'm living and from where I have been, I think there is an expectation that people like me know our place in the Orange state of Northern Ireland."

"You don't strike me as a man who takes kindly to being told his place. Wasn't that what your whole IRA thing was about."

"I suppose. And a fat lot of good that did me too."

"I thought it was others you were doing it for? You know, no more famine graves, no more slums. Isn't that what you dreamed of?"

"Again, not a great deal of success to show there."

"That's always a risk when you stick your head over the parapet."

"I think I'll let others do that in future."

She was quiet for a minute. "So how are you finding Newry?" I asked.

"It's okay," she said.

"Why did you leave Mayo?"

"I felt I was getting into a rut. And my house was filling up with too many bad memories."

I lifted another half-shell. "So, the world is your oyster and Newry is what you choose?"

"I'm a partner in a thriving practice. There's not so many such opportunities for a woman. And it's easier to get to Dublin from Newry rather than Mayo, for when I want to visit my mother."

"Why not Dublin then?"

"Also too many memories there too. Walk down the street and I remember the times I had been there with Charlie when we were at Trinity."

"Grief is the price of love, I suppose."

"Is that supposed to help?"

"Em…"

"Really? My husband lost his life on the Somme and I'm supposed to what… console myself with something trite you picked up from something you've read?"

"There's wisdom in books."

"Maybe. If you're prepared to put what you learn into action for others. Otherwise it's just self-indulgence. And that's what you're doing right now Mick. Being self-indulgent. It's terrible the time you lost in jail. But at least you're alive and that's more than many young men of your generation have. Do you not think that I would give up all the time you lost in prison if it would bring Charlie back for just an hour? But what have you been doing with the life that you have? You're locking yourself up again and have turned your back on a life that you could still live."

"Where did that come from?" I asked.

She looked at me, blinked, and then exhaled. "Sorry Mick. I've been a bit short tempered of late," she said. "I've barely slept this past week with worry about Collette. So, it's not really about what you said. It's just the very sight of you that I find so fucking annoying!"

I felt like I had been thumped in the gut. "You came looking for me. You wanted my help, you said. If you find me that unpalatable why did you bother your arse at all?"

"For fuck sake Mick. You wanted to be a barrister. Look at you now. Cleaning up cow shite in a slaughterhouse."

"Actually it's mostly bullock shite I clean up. Cows produce calves and milk, so you don't want to turn them into stew too often."

"I don't give a fuck about what sort of shite you clean up. You had ambitions. You were going to make the world a better place. What's happened to all of that?"

"Most of it was knocked out of me with some of my teeth."

"Well, you've still got teeth left in your head. So, what are you going to do? Be a good little boy like your Orange masters want? Or try to help build something better."

"What do you suggest?"

"Well, you could finish your degree to start with, the one you didn't finish when you went off gallivanting with the IRA."

"Not got the money for that, I'm afraid."

"Well, you could be saving, couldn't you?"

"I'm not sure that I could ever be called to the bar with the criminal record that I have."

"You could be doing something more than accepting the bullock shite that you are currently shovelling."

She stared at me, her eyes gleaming with fury.

"Look," I said, "I think I need to be going. I'll just get the train back."

She softened slightly. "Don't be silly Mick. I'll take you."

"No that's okay. I'd rather you didn't trouble yourself," I said. And I got up from the table. "I'd like to say it's been a lovely day. But that would hardly be true."

"Mick," she said, but I was already on my way.

"Mick," she said again, but I ignored her. I made the point of paying the bill for our meal on my way out. She can stick her charity up her arse, I thought to myself.

Thursday, 14 May 1925

VII

They were waiting for me as I left work.

I saw two peelers in their bottle green uniforms standing by a Crossley tender as I came out. But they weren't the ones who grabbed me. Two more had been standing to the sides of the abattoir gates and they took me from behind, slamming me against a wall before searching me for weapons. The only thing I had on me was a jack knife but they took it anyway before cuffing me and then bundling me towards their truck.

"What's this about?" I managed to ask.

"Shut the fuck up."

"Where are you taking me?"

"Say one more word, you Fenian bastard, and you'll be sorry."

I said nothing more. But they gave me a proper kicking when they got me in the back of the lorry anyway.

VIII

Along with my watch and the contents of my pockets, they took my belt and my boots and stuck me in a cell that was bare of all furniture apart from a chamber pot. There was no lighting and no glass in the tiny, barred window. It was Baltic cold. I spent the night shivering, huddled in the corner to try to keep warm.

I must have drifted off for a bit because I was awakened by the sound of boots stomping down the corridor and a jangling of keys. The door creaked open and in the dawn's watery light I saw two big peelers entering my cell. Expecting another onslaught of boots I instinctively pushed myself to my feet.

"Turn around!" the bigger of the two said. He had a strong east Belfast accent and carried himself with the bearing of a soldier. I guessed he was a veteran of the Ulster Volunteer Force and had probably warmed up for the pogroms in Belfast with service in France in the 36th Ulster Division.

I did as I was told. "Hands behind your back," he said.

Again, I said nothing and complied. I felt the cold steel of the cuffs as he manacled me. Then he and his pal grabbed me by the arms and frog-marched me out of the cell, down the corridor and up a couple of flights of stairs.

We arrived on a landing lit by gas. It was blessedly warmer here than it had been in the cells. They led me to the end of the corridor and to a door with a name neatly lettered in black and gold on the translucent glass: Inspector Robert

Hanby. The east Belfast man knocked and we heard a barked order: "ENTER!"

The east Belfast man opened the door and I was pushed through.

Inside behind a wooden desk sat a strongly built, uniformed and heavily moustachioed man, who I presumed was Hanby. He had a cigarette in his mouth and was shuffling papers into a folder. He looked up at me as he tapped the edge of the folder on the desk and set it into an out-tray. Then he picked another folder from an in-tray, opened it and began leafing through the pages it contained.

"Thanks Jeffrey. You can leave him with me now and get yourselves some breakfast. I'll give you a bell when I need you."

"Right Inspector," the east Belfast man said, and tramped out of the office closing the door behind him. I had neither eaten nor drunk anything in 12 hours, so the thought of breakfast set my stomach rumbling, which is probably why the inspector said it.

Hanby said nothing further for a while, carefully perusing the pages that he now had in front of him as he smoked. Finally he looked up. "You can sit," he said, gesturing to the wooden chair in front of his desk. I sat down on the chair and regretted it almost immediately. As I still had my hands cuffed behind my back I only managed half an arse on the seat. It had been more comfortable standing.

"So, Michael Gerard McAlinden," he said, making a show of reading from his folder. He had a local accent, but it had a distinctly Protestant timbre.

"Late of the so-called West Mayo Flying Column," he went on. "That was a long way to go to murder loyal subjects of the Crown wasn't it?"

I thought of telling him to fuck off but I decided to try to keep to what I hoped was dignified silence.

"It wasn't all fun and games though was it? Islandeady— three of your comrades killed when the Tommies you wanted to ambush ambushed you. And I bet you wonder why they tell Paddy jokes over the water. And Kilmeena—that was seven-two to the Black and Tans wasn't it? My oh my. That must have smarted, having to turn tail and run from the likes of them."

"We paid them back in the same coin at Carrowkennedy." I knew I should have kept my mouth shut. But it was clear that the career of the West Mayo Flying Column was not news to him.

"I see that. Eight Black and Tans killed and sixteen captured."

"I know. We counted them."

"How many did you account for?"

"That I was not counting."

"Just shooting and scooting?"

"You've been in a few fights I would imagine, Inspector."

"I have."

"Well, you know then, don't you?"

"Aye. Though some of you are always pretty sure about when you have to go hand to hand with bayonets." Hanby took another long puff on his cigarette. "I'm curious to see you didn't shoot the prisoners though," he went on.

"Why so? Haven't you heard of the Hague Conventions?"

"Ah yes, you're a drop out from the law aren't you? So, did you school your comrades on the international law of war?"

"You don't have to know the law to be decent human beings."

The inspector snorted. "Forgive me," he said. "But I have not found decency in great supply in the ranks of the IRA. So, I'll reserve my judgement for the moment." He returned to his notes. "Picked up in August 1922 in South Armagh, and, until a couple of months ago you've been enjoying the hospitality of His Majesty. You must count yourself lucky. Times were that traitors like you were hung from the nearest tree."

"Aye. Now you just shoot them down in their homes."

"You think you have the moral high ground to raise that sort of thing given those you've been associating with these past few years?"

I said nothing.

He closed the folder and gave me an appraising look.

"What am I doing here, Inspector?"

"Anthony McCreevy," Hanby said.

"What about him?"

"Your remarkably chatty for an IRA man. I'd have thought you would go with 'Who?' when I mentioned that name."

"I met him once. Seemed liked a decent lad."

"So why were you seen threatening him this Saturday past."

"Who told you that?" I asked.

"Ah now Michael. The way it works is I'm the one who asks the questions."

"I wasn't threatening him. Just had a chat with him."

"Again, not what I heard."

"Well, someone is telling you shite then."

By now I wished I had followed my own advice on interrogations and just kept my gob shut. I didn't know what this peeler's deal was, but I already felt uneasy about the way the conversation was going.

"Why were you talking to him?" Hanby asked.

"What's going on here, Inspector? Having ill-tempered words with someone is all of a sudden a criminal offence?"

"So you admit they were ill-tempered?"

"I think the young fella might have misunderstood something that I said."

"Why were you speaking to him at all."

"I just bumped into him when I was out."

"Was that when you got those injuries to your face?"

I managed a laugh. "Inspector, I presume you have never been arrested by your own constables."

Hanby grunted a laugh. "I know some of the lads think it is their duty to put manners on suspects, soften them up, to make them a bit more cooperative when the likes of me chat to them," Hanby said. "But those injuries to your face are older than last night."

"I had a bit of a disagreement with someone over the weekend. What? Is Anthony saying we had a fight?"

"Anthony is not saying much these days. He's dead."

That gave me a start. "What?" I managed to croak.

"Found on Thursday morning in a field in Dromintee. Hands tied behind his back. Bullet to the back of his head. Not the first such killing like that we have seen. So naturally our first thoughts were of the IRA. And then our second thoughts,

56

given what we heard about the run in that you had with Anthony on Saturday, was you."

"Why on God's earth would I want to kill him. Sure he was only a child."

"Why indeed? But at the moment we don't even know why you were talking to him in the first place so you'll understand if I am not wholly satisfied with your account of events so far."

We looked at each other. The silence gathered for a few moments.

"Where were you on Wednesday?"

"I was at work until five and then I went home."

"Who can confirm that?"

"Anybody at work. And my mother and father."

"Forgive me if I don't find an alibi from the family of an IRA man convincing."

"It's the truth."

"Did you go out Wednesday evening?"

"I had my dinner and went out for a pint."

"Where did you go for the pint?"

"Armagh side of Jonesborough."

"How did you get there?"

"I cycled."

"What time were you home at?"

"Towards midnight."

"Who can confirm that?"

"The barman in the pub. But I don't know his name."

"So you just sat in the pub talking to no one?"

"With the summer evenings you are able to read."

"You aren't able to read at home?"

"They don't have porter there."

"What are you reading?"

"*Don Quixote*."

"What's it about?"

"Two fellas wandering around Spain, talking shite."

"Well, that's appropriate isn't it? Here's the two of us here this morning and you're talking nothing but shite."

"I'm telling you the truth." At least some of it, I thought.

"Dromintee is not far from Jonesborough."

"It's not. But I did not go to Dromintee."

"How did you get those injuries on your face?"

"I told you. I got into a bit of a disagreement with someone over the weekend."

"Who?"

"It was the first time I met the fella."

"Did he have a name?"

"I can't really recall."

"Fuck's sake," said Hanby.

I said nothing.

"Look," said Hanby, "with your background I know you are not likely to be given to be trusting of the peelers. But I promise you it is in your own best interests to quit fucking me around with this horseshite story of yours and tell me what the fuck you were up to at the weekend with Anthony McCreevy. Because as it stands you look good for this killing. And whether you did it or not is not the greatest of bothers to me. You did some things that you should still be inside for. And even if the powers-that-be saw fit to let you out, I think it would be natural justice for you to be back inside. And if they hang you, that is, again, no great bother to me. I have seen better men than you die for less."

I shifted on my chair. I am not going to lie. Along with the physical discomfort I was beginning to worry. This cop was certainly convincing that he would like nothing better than to throw away the key on me.

"So," Hanby went on, "start talking."

"I would like to see a solicitor."

"I would like to see Louise Brooks for midnight cocktails in Paris. But we don't always get what we want now do we?"

"I'm bound by some professional confidences."

"You're a fucking labourer in an abattoir. You have no professional responsibilities to fucking anyone."

"I didn't say I was the professional in this situation."

"Who else then?"

"It would help if I could speak to a solicitor."

"Not going to happen."

"I have rights."

"And I have the Emergency Powers Act. So your rights can go fuck themselves."

"I could do with a doctor then. I was pissing some blood this morning following your goons softening up yesterday."

"Then I would suggest that you start answering my questions otherwise you will be pissing some more blood before long. Jeffery and Ian will just be finishing their breakfast. They'll be brimming up with energy for the new day by now."

It seemed like a stalemate. I really didn't want to be spending any more time inside. So I could think of nothing else to say.

"Dr Sophia Hennessy."

"Who the fuck is that?"

"She's a doctor in town. She is a partner in a practice on the Belfast Road. If you speak to her she may be able to explain what I was doing on Saturday. I don't want to say anything more in case I betray her professional confidences."

"I'll say it again. This is why the English keep telling those Paddy jokes. Through sheer stupidity you do insist on making life hard for yourselves."

Hanby pressed a button on the wall and in the distance I heard a bell ring, followed shortly after by the clump of hobnail boots on the corridor outside. They paused outside and there was a knock at the door.

"ENTER," shouted Hanby.

The door opened and it was Constable Jeffery standing there. "Yes Inspector?"

"Take Mr McAlinden here back to the cells. And take good care of him along the way. He's thought a bit of a celebrity in some parts you know. For killing policemen."

IX

For a big ugly bastard Constable Jeffery was not as stupid as he looked. He certainly knew how to take a hint. So he delayed taking me back to my cell for just long enough to grab Constable Ian and for the two of them to give me another pounding in the police toilets on the corridor below Hanby's office. All fists this time, so I suppose for that at least I should have been grateful.

Afterwards, they dumped me back in the cell, which at least had gotten a little warmer as the morning had worn on. Someone had emptied my chamber pot so the smell was a bit improved too, and after a short while someone delivered me a mug of black tea. I thought it best to not to think about the spit content of the tea and instead appreciate that someone had added a couple of sugars. It is the nature of tea, in any form, to always make you feel a bit more human. This was, I was aware, a sign that I was getting back into a prison mode of thinking that I was beginning to count these as blessings.

I spent much of the rest of the morning doing circuits of my cell, not least to keep warm. After an hour or so of that I sat again in what I had come to regard as my favourite corner and dozed for a while.

I was awakened by the now familiar heavy clump of boots and the scrapping of keys in the lock. Again I pushed myself to my feet and waited until they shackled me and then allowed myself to be led back up the stairs to Hanby's office.

I noticed through the window that there was a clear blue sky outside but the light suggested that it was getting towards evening. I really had no idea what time it was.

"Sit down," said Hanby.

"I think I'll stay standing."

"Suit yourself," said Hanby. He leaned back in his chair and lit a cigarette, took a long draw and then exhaled a cloud of blue smoke.

"Well," he said, "you do like to make things hard for yourself."

"Not as much as your gorillas."

"You can hardly be surprised can you? Given what the police have had to put up with here these past couple of years."

"It's been tough all over I think you'll find," I said.

"All over is not my responsibility," Hanby said. "However, this portion of south Ulster is. So, I do not need uppity Fenians like you threatening the tenuous peace we have come to enjoy in these parts."

"You might call it peace," I said. "Others will call it desolation."

"Tacitus."

"Yes," I said.

"Just think what you could have done with all that learning if you hadn't decided to devote your life to killing your Protestant neighbours instead."

"I have only ever fired on foreign mercenaries, not on neighbours." That wasn't quite true. But I thought if Hanby knew any better he would have brought it up by now.

"Well, there are no foreign mercenaries, as you call them, in these parts, so I would advise you to keep your nose clean from here on."

I said nothing.

"So, I don't mind telling you that you've been a pain in my arse today, McAlinden."

"I didn't ask for this shite."

"You've not offered much help in digging yourself out of it though have you?"

Again I said nothing.

"I've been to see your Doctor Hennessy. Easy on the eye, isn't she? I mean, for a ginger."

He watched me for a reaction. "She tells me you were assisting her with an enquiry about a patient that she was concerned about," Hanby went one. "Too hard for you to have told me that earlier?"

"Like I said, it was her confidence I was keeping. I didn't think it would be ethical for me to say something."

"Ethical? Your lot see nothing wrong with dragging elderly Protestants out of their beds to murder them in the dark of night. But you draw the line at telling me you were on a joy-ride with a redhead?"

This was becoming tiresome. But I decided not to say anything lest it gather another kicking from Hanby's untamed peelers.

"She had some interesting information though, did your Doctor Hennessy."

I said nothing.

"Not interested? She told me who did that to your face."

I tried to look impassive, but Hanby's comment made me nervous. Hoey was a repellent bastard but, even so, old habits die hard and I was uneasy about being open to any accusation of being an informer. Even at one step removed.

"Yes, we know a lot about Cathal Hoey, but didn't know he was back in these parts. I heard he was down South for a bit in that Civil War they had. But now he's back. Just inside the Free State where he knows we can't get our hands on him for some of the things he's done. A bad bastard if ever there was one."

Hanby took another drag on his cigarette. It was my experience that there were a lot of bad bastards about but that they rarely thought of themselves as such. Instead they thought themselves warriors in the cause of righteousness. That was why they could bring themselves to do the dark and bloody things that they did. I suspected Hanby might be one such. I sometimes wondered if that was what I also had become.

"You know something?" Hanby asked. I presumed it was a rhetorical question so I said nothing. "The happiest year of my life was watching you Fenians tearing lumps out of each other for the privilege of presiding over the collapse of that poxy Free State. So I must admit Dr Hennessy telling me how Hoey kicked the shite out of you quite cheered me up." He gave me a sneering smile and stubbed out the butt of his fag. "Yes, indeed. Just the sort of news to set me up for the weekend."

He picked up a fountain pen and signed a paper that was on a blotter before him. "Under the Emergency Powers Act I could keep you for another couple of days and let you fester over the weekend. But because you've given me a bit of a chuckle I'm going to let you go. For now. But don't go anywhere. We may want another word or two with you. And behave yourself unless you like the look of the inside of a police cell." He rang the bell by his desk again and a different peeler from Ugly Jeffrey showed up.

"Give Mr McAlinden here back his boots and his belt and get him out of here," Hanby instructed the minion.

Twenty minutes later, newly belted and booted, I was escorted out the door of the barracks and shoved unceremoniously back onto the street. I took a deep breath and wiped my face. They'd given me back my watch but not my jack knife. I'd liked that knife but not enough to get into a fracas with the peelers about it.

It was past six in the evening I noticed as I fastened my returned watch around my wrist. I wondered if my bicycle was still safe outside the abattoir, otherwise I had a long walk home ahead of me. I started down the street.

I was startled by the beep of a car horn behind me. I turned. Sophia was behind the wheel. She waved when I saw her, opened her car door and made to get out. I walked back towards her.

"How are you, Mick?"

There was a look of concern on her face. "Not too bad," I said. "Cold and hungry but only two kickings so I shouldn't complain."

"Jesus, Mick. I'm so sorry."

"Aye. I think you should be." If I hadn't gone off gallivanting with her on Saturday I would not have been picked up. So, as I had decided in the police cell, I would set aside all reason and conclude that this was all her fault.

"I had a nice life, you know, cleaning up cow shite. Maybe not what you'd call a success, but not so many of the kickings from the peelers." At least, I thought, this did afford me a degree of passive aggressive vengeance for her harsh words when last we spoke.

For a moment I thought she was going to blub and felt a pang of regret. But she didn't. She just said "Sorry," again.

Then, "Can I take you anywhere? Do you want to get something to eat."

"No," I said, and then added, "thank you." She must have been waiting a good while outside the police barracks, and it sounded like it was her good Protestant word that had got me out of there.

"I need to be getting home," I said. "My mother will be worrying."

"I can run you up the road."

"I need to pick up my bike."

"Won't it be there in the morning, after you've had your dinner and a good night's sleep?"

If I had not felt so bone weary Sophia's argument might not have resonated just so deeply. "You make a good point," I said. "And it's a very kind offer. Thank you." I moved to the passenger side door and got in. Sophia got in herself and started her engine. Checking her mirrors, she moved smoothly into the street.

"How long had you been waiting?" I asked.

"About an hour," she said. "That inspector, Hanby, came to see me a bit earlier. I said that if he didn't release you immediately after what I told him that I would be round with a solicitor. Whatever the Emergency Powers Act says, I don't think he fancied the hassle. Anyway, I followed him here and told him I would be waiting."

"I was a bit surprised to be let out, I must admit. He could have had me festering for the weekend."

Sophia paused at a junction to check for approaching vehicles.

"So, Anthony McCreevy is dead," she said.

"So I'm informed."

"Do the police know who did it?"

"Hanby says his first thoughts turned to me. I am not sure he believes that anymore. On the other hand, if he could pin it on me I don't think it would trouble his conscience mightily if he put me away for it."

"How can he justify that attitude?"

"As far as he's concerned even if I haven't killed Anthony, I've probably killed enough loyal servants of the Crown that I should never see the light of day again."

Sophia was quiet for a moment, and then asked, "Did you do much of that in the flying column?"

I thought for a moment about what to say. I was too tired to think up something cleverly evasive so I decided to go with the truth. "I've definitely killed one man, and I've tried to kill maybe a half dozen more in the fights I was in. Not sure what the results of all the shooting was. But I suppose from Hanby's perspective, he has a point."

We were silent for a while, until we were at the edge of the town now and starting up the Dublin Road. I decided that I must seem pretty morose to someone who was going a couple of miles out of her way to see me home. "So," I asked, "how's your week been? Get anywhere with your own detective work?"

Sophia gave me a sidewards glance. "Well," she said, "I found out some stuff."

Part Two: Sophia

Monday 11 May 1925

X

"I'd like to speak to the auxiliary bishop, please."

Sophia had spent the morning preoccupied about Collette, finding little distraction in the routine of her general practice. Finally, at lunchtime she had told her colleagues that she needed to take the afternoon to deal with some personal matters. Her appointment schedule was relatively light that day so she didn't think it was too much of an imposition to ask her partners to take the extra couple of patients.

Once that had been arranged she set off up the road to Belfast to speak to a man she thought might be able to get some nuns to open up to her.

"Can I ask what this is related to?"

The bishop's secretary sitting before her now was a priest. He was young and clean shaven with impeccably manicured nails and smelling vaguely of lavender water. He might have been good-looking if he didn't have such a supercilious air of pomposity about him. This was a man, Sophia imagined, who knew he was on the fast track to power and would enjoy lording it over every underling who ever had the misfortune to pass under his nose.

"It's a confidential matter," Sophia said.

"Well, I'm afraid his Eminence has a very busy schedule for the rest of the day. He is preparing for confirmations later this evening."

"I won't need to speak to him for long."

"I may be able to squeeze you in to see him next week if you would like to come back then?"

"I'm afraid the matter is rather more urgent than that."

"This is quite irregular."

"I'm really sorry," Sophia said. "Perhaps if you could just tell him that it is Doctor Sophia Hennessy and I need to see him about a professional matter."

The priest looked at her up and down. It was not any sort of sexual appraisal, Sophia thought, but rather a snobbish one: he was trying to work out if she was important enough for him to be bothered with.

"What sort of doctor are you? Philosophy?"

"I'm a medical doctor," said Sophia.

And those were the magic words. He let out a sigh. "Please take a seat," he said, indicating to a couple of chairs against the wall, "and I will see if his Eminence can speak to you."

Sophia turned towards the chairs as the priest arose from his own seat. His footsteps echoed on the dark timber floor as he approached another door which he quietly knocked and entered. He was barely a minute inside before the door opened again and the young priest called towards her. "Please come this way," he said.

The room that Sophia was ushered into was a bright office with two of the walls lined with books and a large crucifix overhanging a flower adorned alter occupying a third.

Windows looking out onto a neatly kept garden filled the fourth wall. The office's only occupant was already out from behind his desk moving towards her with an outstretched hand. "Doctor Hennessy. So good to see you!" said Martin Crosby, auxiliary bishop of the Diocese of Down and Connor.

Sophia took his hand. "So good of you to see me, your Eminence. Particularly at such short notice."

"Could you organise us some tea, Paul?" the bishop said to the young priest who was still hovering at the door. "Or would you prefer coffee?" he asked Sophia.

"Would you recommend it?"

"I would! Belfast has a large Italian community, one of whom we have been fortunate enough to have as our housekeeper here. So, it's good stuff."

"Coffee then would be lovely."

"Thanks, Paul."

The two of them watched as Fr Paul closed the door, then turned back towards each other.

"Sophia," said the bishop.

"Martin."

"How long has it been?"

"Three years. Since they promoted you away from Mayo. How are you finding Belfast? An urban setting must suit a city boy like yourself better than the wilds of Connaught?"

"Well, it's not Dublin. And I know I'm cosseted here, but it's been a difficult time. The Catholic population of the city has had it very bad these past few years. The Northern Ireland government has turned its dogs loose upon them and cried 'Havoc'."

"Yes, I've read the papers. I'm glad not to be living here."

"Please, have a seat." He gestured to a chair and he resumed his place behind his desk.

"So, where are you now? Newry, I think I heard?"

"Indeed, Newry. It's fine. It's not the prettiest town in Ireland, but the countryside around it is stunning."

It was a while since Sophia had had a conversation like this. One that was essentially about nothing because what was unsaid was too painful.

"Do you miss Mayo?"

"A bit. But there were too many memories and nothing to keep me really."

"I see," said Crosby. "Why Newry though?"

"It was an opportunity. A friend from Trinity thought that a woman doctor might help his practice expand."

"There was that young fella in Mayo, do you remember... what was his name? He came from around Newry didn't he?"

Sophia felt a pang of regret at the way her conversation with Mick had ended the Saturday just passed. "Mick McAlinden you mean?"

"That's him! What ever became of him did you hear?"

"I saw him in Newry. He's just got out of jail."

"That can't have been much fun. But I suppose he's luckier than many. What's he up to now?"

"He's working in an abattoir."

"Wasn't he a law student?"

"Yes. But I think prison rather disrupted his longer-term career plans."

"Well, at least he is still alive, so I suppose there is always hope."

There was a soft knock at the door and a dark-eyed woman with black hair and olive skin entered bearing a tray and the aroma of coffee.

"This is Mrs Pavonne, who I was telling you about," Crosby said.

"Lovely to meet you, Mrs Pavonne," said Sophia.

The woman looked up briefly and smiled at Sophia as she set the tray down on a corner of Martin's desk. She poured coffee from a small pot into two cups and doctored one for Martin with frothing hot milk, before setting the milk and sugar before Sophia so that she could adjust her cup to her own taste. Sophia just added some of the milk. "Thank you," she said.

"You are most welcome," said Mrs Pavonne in Italian accented English, and she gathered up the accoutrements onto the tray and left the room. Sophia watched her until the door closed behind her.

"So," said Crosby. "Lovely as it is to see you and catch up on old times, but what is it has brought you here?"

"I need some help?"

"What sort of help?"

"I have a patient. She is pregnant. But she has gone missing. Everyone I ask tells me to mind my own business."

"I see," said Crosby. "May I ask, was she a married lady?"

"No."

"So, what age of a girl are we talking about?"

"She's fourteen."

"Aha," said Crosby.

"What does 'Aha' mean?" asked Sophia.

"She's probably gone off to the Sisters to have the baby."

"The who now?"

"How long have you been a doctor, Sophia? You must have heard of this before?"

"Heard of what exactly?"

"Sometimes, if a girl becomes pregnant out of wedlock, the family sends her off to a convent run by one of the orders of nuns to have the child. The sisters take care of her and the family avoid the shame."

"And what happens once the baby arrives?"

"The nuns will often arrange adoption for a loving family that can't have children of their own."

Sophia took a sip of her coffee. It was indeed lovely.

"So, if this is all so benign, why the wall of silence."

"What do you mean?"

"Her school headmistress told me in no uncertain terms to get lost. Her Da told me he'd kill me if I came round asking questions again."

"That does sound a bit extreme."

"He was IRA. But I suspect he was a mean bastard even before that."

"Still."

"Indeed."

Crosby said nothing and took a sip from his own coffee cup. "I don't know why people are so defensive. Perhaps it's because you're an outsider. Perhaps it's because you're a Protestant. For an area with very few Protestants, the IRA in South Armagh have had some considerable taint of sectarianism on them."

"I had an IRA man with me the last time I saw the father. It did not seem to help with the trust much."

"Where did you get one of them?"

"Mick McAlinden. I told you I met him in Newry."

76

"Well, that came in handy."

"Not as much as I had hoped." She sipped some more coffee. "So, how do I get to see her?"

"Why do you need to do that? Sure many of the nuns are nurses and will have their own doctors to take care of her."

"Well, I could tell you that my concern is principally professional. I would like to make sure that she is in good hands before I close the book on her, so to speak. But the thing is, I promised her that things would be okay. My heart went out to her when I met her. She is a bright girl with great promise. But she was terrified, particularly of her father. And I promised her that things would be okay. So I would like to try to keep my promise."

"But she's safe now. She is with the nuns."

"I've heard a few stories about nuns."

"Some of them can be a bit unpleasant. But many of them are lovely, dedicated women."

"Lovely to a bishop. Might be different with a pregnant girl. People abuse power."

"Fools abuse power," said Crosby.

"Well, I suspect you may have a fool in your outer office then." Crosby snorted a laugh.

"Like us all, he has his flaws. But I think he is a man with promise. We'll see how he gets on after his next appointment."

"You have that planned already?"

"Well, it's confidential of course, but between you and me, there is a parish on the Lower Falls that could, I think, benefit from the attentions of a man like Father Paul there. I'm certain he would benefit from being there too, give him some real pastoral challenges, not just diary scheduling problems."

"I'm glad to hear you are thinking of such things, Martin. But can you do anything to help me? Please."

Crosby sipped some of his coffee. "I suppose I could write a few letters, make a few phone calls."

"That would be great Martin. I would really, really appreciate that."

Crosby picked up a notebook and pen from his desk and handed it to Sophia. "Name of the girl, parents' names, address, date of birth if you have it, and any distinguishing features." Sophia started scribbling.

"Also the name of her school, and do you know the name of the headmistress there?" Crosby asked.

"It was Sister Conceptua."

"Grand. Write that down too. And do you have a phone number yourself?"

"There is a phone at my practise."

"Write that down and I'll be in touch if I find out anything so."

Sophia finished writing and proffered the notebook and pen to Crosby as she stood. His fingers brushed hers. For a second she felt that old spark of heat and a memory came unbidden of how those fingers had once traced the contours of her skin in the candlelit darkness long ago.

"Thank you, Martin," she said, and before any more inconvenient memories erupted, she propelled herself through the door and out into the cool of the foyer.

XI

Sophia paused at her car door long enough to retrieve a cigarette from her bag. She had difficulty lighting it because her hands were shaking. Eventually she managed to spark up and breathed in the smoke deeply until she felt the nicotine calming her. She wondered if some wounds ever heal.

She finished the cigarette and ground it underneath the toe of her boot. Then she drove back to Newry as the darkness began to settle around her.

Friday 15 May 1925

XII

Sophia followed Mick's directions and drove up the Dublin Road and then along a couple of winding roads that led to his family home in Killean. It was a neat, white-washed cottage with black trim and a black slate roof. It was set back from the road with a large yard before it, several sheds to the side, and a cluster of barns behind it. The sound of her car as she turned into the yard seemed to stir some life in the house and the door opened. A middle-aged couple and a young man emerged as Sophia brought her car to a halt.

Mick opened the door of the car and jumped out.

"God be praised," said the woman and she started to cry.

"Don't worry Ma," said Mick, "I'm still in one piece," and he folded her into a hug as she continued to sob. The older man, placed his arms around the two of them and the young man slapped Mick on the back.

Sophia waited until the embrace broke and Mick turned back towards her. She waved and put her car into gear. Family time, she thought.

Mick raised his hand to signal her to wait and approached her side of the car. She opened her window. "You're going to have to say hello."

"I don't want to intrude," said Sophia.

"Ach, don't talk oul shite," said Mick, and he opened her door. Sophia switched off her engine, put on the handbrake and got out.

"This is my mother," said Mick, ushering the woman towards Sophia. "Ma, this is Dr Hennessy."

"Just call me Sophia. Lovely to meet you Mrs McAlinden."

"Eilish," said Mrs McAlinden. "Thanks for bringing my son home."

"Sure it was nothing," said Sophia. "Just a wee run up the road."

"It was not nothing," said Mick. "Sophia saw me right with the peelers. If she hadn't stuck her oar in with them I think I would still be cooling my heels inside Newry police barracks." Then turning to bring his father forward, "This is my Da, Gerry," said Mick.

"Pleasure to meet you, Dr Hennessy," said Gerry.

"Likewise. And it's Sophia, please."

"And this fella is my big brother, Joe."

Joe must have been three inches taller that Mick and broader again. He extended his hand, "Pleasure to meet you, Sophia."

"Sure the pleasure is all mine," said Sophia as she took his hand. "Mick said you were his big brother. I thought he just meant older."

"He's four years younger than me and half a foot shorter," said Joe. But, thought Sophia, Mick already looked five years older.

"Is that everyone?" asked Sophia.

"We've a sister, Ursula, who is three years older than Mick," said Joe, "but she is married and living in Meigh."

"Nice to have all your family so close," said Sophia.

"It is, though this one," Eilish nodded to Mick, "has given us a few frights. We thought that was a thing of the past, but no, in trouble with the police again."

"So what happened?" asked Gerry.

"Did you hear young Anthony McCreevy was found dead a couple of days ago?" Mick asked.

"We did," said Gerry.

"The peelers thought that gave them the excuse to pick me up. Give me a going over for old time sake, like."

"Fuck sake," said Joe.

"I know," said Mick.

"Well, come in now," said Eilish, "and we'll get youse something to eat."

"I'll say goodbye then," said Sophia.

"You will not," said Eilish. "You'll stay and have something to eat. It's the least we can do."

"I don't want to intrude," said Sophia.

"No intrusion," said Gerry. "It would be our pleasure."

So, the five of them trooped into the house and Sophia was settled at the place of honour at the head of the kitchen table.

"Will you take a wee drink?" asked Gerry.

"What do you have?" asked Sophia.

"We have whiskey," said Gerry.

"And there is still that brandy from Christmas," said Eilish.

"I'd take a wee brandy then," said Sophia.

Gerry served her the drink in a cut glass goblet, and poured another for Eilish, while Eilish dispatched Joe to get turf for the fire and Mick was sent to get washed up, while she started preparing the food.

"Thank you so much for taking Mick home," said Gerry as he sat down at the table with a small glass of whiskey in his hand which he touched to the rim of Sophia's glass.

"It was the least I could do," said Sophia. "I'm afraid I think that he got into trouble with the police because of me."

"How so?" asked Gerry.

"He was helping me with an enquiry about a patient, which led us to have a conversation with that young McCreevy fella who was killed."

"Ach, Sophia. With Mick's record the police will use any excuse. If it hadn't been this, it would have been something else. I heard tell of one ex-IRA fella from town who was given a package by a Protestant neighbour to deliver to somebody in Belfast. The fella had enough gumption to look inside and found it was a revolver and ammunition. So he dumped it. Then as soon as he arrived in Belfast he was stopped and searched by the police. So it was a set up."

"Still, I can't help feeling a bit guilty about what happened to Mick."

"Sure what is done is done. And you've brought him home now."

They drank their drinks for a moment, and Sophia savoured the tang of the brandy on her palate.

"It's a while since I've had brandy," said Sophia. "I normally stick with the whiskey if I am having a spirit."

"It's never too late to change if you like," said Gerry.

"No, this is lovely. It's a nice change."

Mick came back into the kitchen, clean shaven and in a fresh shirt. "Thank God for that," said Gerry, "you were smelling like a dirty sock there for a bit."

Mick smiled and sat down. "Feeling a bit more human now."

"Do you want a cup of tea?" asked Gerry.

"I'd prefer one of those," said Mick, nodding towards Gerry's whiskey glass.

"I think that can be arranged," said Gerry, and he stood up and walked to a dresser against the kitchen wall. "I think the occasion demands some Waterford crystal," and he lifted down a couple more cut-glass whiskey tumblers from the shelves.

"Jaysus," said Mick. "Are you feeling okay, Da?"

"The prodigal has returned," said Gerry. "But don't be getting used to it."

Gerry placed the lead crystal before Mick and poured a generous measure of whiskey for him. "Welcome home, son," he said, and raised his glass. The three of them touched their glasses.

"*Sláinte*," said Sophia.

"*Sláinte*," said Mick and Gerry in unison.

"Mick says you are only recently moved to Newry," said Gerry.

"That's right. I used to live in Mayo. That's where I met Mick."

"When was that?" Gerry asked.

"It must have been 1920 or 21, was it Mick?"

"1920," said Mick, "just before I joined the flying column."

"We've never been to Mayo," said Eilish from where she was working at the stove.

"It's beautiful," said Sophia. "But I fancied a change of scene after a while."

"So how are you finding Newry?" asked Gerry.

"It's grand. The work is good and the coffee is better than where I was in Mayo."

"It's hardly the bright lights of Dublin though, is it?" asked Gerry.

"It's not. But I can get that every now and then when I go to visit my mother."

"So she's still alive?"

"She is. But my father died a year ago, so she is pining a bit for him."

"Ach that's very sad," said Gerry. "What age of a man was he?"

"He was seventy."

"A brave age," said Eilish, "but you'd still wish he was a bit older wouldn't you?"

"I would," said Sophia, "but that is the way of all things isn't it? And he had a good life, so that is something."

"What did he do?" asked Gerry.

"He was a doctor too. A surgeon in Dublin."

"You are following in his footsteps then," said Eilish.

"Sort of. But a lot of surgeons would think the work of general practice was beneath them."

"Sure what do them oul eejits know?" said Eilish, as she set a pot of tea on the table.

Joe arrived back with the turf, some of which he fed into the stove and the rest he piled in a basket to one side. Then, over the next half an hour, Eilish prepared a huge fry up for them all with fresh soda bread. She apologised as she served, "Sure if I had known we were going to have guests I would have made something nice."

"Sure there's fewer things nicer than a bit of bacon," said Sophia.

"Which one was this?" asked Joe.

"This one was Oliver Cromwell," said Gerry.

It took Sophia a moment to register what Gerry was saying. "You mean you named your pig, Oliver Cromwell?" she asked.

"I did," said Gerry. "You should always know what you eat."

"Do all your pigs have names?"

"Just the ones that we are going to butcher and eat ourselves," said Gerry.

"I heard tell once," said Sophia, "of a French woman who would name the lobsters that she wanted to eat after her ex-husbands. She said it made it easier for her to toss them into the boiling water."

"She sounds like a woman after my own heart," said Gerry.

"Your heart is no longer your own," said Eilish, "so don't go day-dreaming about any gay French divorcees."

Gerry laughed but said no more.

"Next month," said Joe, "We'll be tucking into Winston Churchill."

"I think I might save Churchill for another month or so," said Gerry. "The amount of lard on him makes him more of a beast for winter eating. No, I think it will be Charles Trevelyan for the chop next."

"That has to be the best name ever for a pig," said Sophia. Trevelyan was knighted by Queen Victoria for overseeing, on behalf of the British government, the deaths of a million Irish people during the Famine and the exile of a million more.

"It is," said Gerry. "So his death will be an historic moment."

"How so?" Mick asked.

"It'll be the first time a Charles Trevelyan will ever have fed the hungry in Ireland."

"Let's see what sort of black pudding the blackguard makes," said Eilish. "But before we get to that, I have a Victoria sponge I made this afternoon if anybody would like a piece?"

The suggestion met with general approval from the table. "Well, clear up those dinner plates then, Mick," said Eilish, "and I'll get the cake."

Mick stood. The plates were passed to him and he carried them to the sink.

"Would you like some more tea, Sophia?" asked Joe.

"I would," said Sophia.

Joe lifted the pot and was just about to fill Sophia's cup when Gerry shouted at him. "In the name of Jaysus, son!"

"What?" asked Joe.

"Do you want Doctor Hennessy to think that we are all savages here?"

"What do you mean?" asked Joe.

"That tea must be near an hour old. Go off and make a fresh pot!"

Sheepishly Joe murmured, "A hundred thousand apologies, Sophia. I'll make you some fresh tea now," and he shuffled off towards the kitchen sink to fill a fresh kettle.

"You try to raise them right," said Gerry, "and then something like that happens, makes you question every choice you have ever made."

"I don't know, Gerry," said Sophia. "It looks to me like you have done all right with the two of them."

Gerry looked at his family milling around the far end of the kitchen, bickering happily as they made the tea and washed the plates. He lowered his voice then.

"Mick has been a worry though. That time he was in Mayo put years on both myself and Eilish and he was not the same when he came back. There was a darkness about him that wasn't there before. I don't know what things were like in Mayo, but I dread the thought that he was involved there in some of the same sort of stuff that went on around here."

"Did you ever talk to him about it?"

"I've been afraid to," said Gerry, "afraid of what he might tell me."

Sophia took a sip of her brandy. "I honestly don't know Gerry. But even the most honourable war, if there ever is such a thing, can leave a dreadful mark on even the most honourable of men. I remember my husband, Charlie, when he was on leave from France during the war. It had changed him too. Some of the things he saw. Some of the things he had done. It left an awful melancholy about him."

"How is he now?" asked Gerry.

"He's still in France. He fell at the Somme."

"God that's awful sad. I'm sorry for your loss."

"Thank you," said Sophia. "But we were talking about your son, not my husband. And I think you must just trust that where there is life there is hope."

"I believe that," said Gerry, glancing over at Mick. "And they also say time is a great healer."

"Well," said Sophia, "one out of two isn't bad."

Joe arrived back with the fresh tea, followed swiftly by Eilish carrying the cake and a large knife and Mick with a fist full of piece plates and cutlery which he distributed around the table as Joe poured the tea and Eilish portioned out the sponge.

"This is such a treat," said Sophia. "I normally only have cake when I am out for coffee."

"You don't bake yourself, Sophia?" asked Eilish.

"No. I'm more of a cook than a baker. Not that I have much time for that anymore, what with work."

"Your mother didn't teach you."

"My mother thought such things were beneath her. So she had a lovely girl from Kerry working for us, who kept us fed. She used to take care of me in the kitchen when my parents were away and taught me some rudiments. Then there was a French girl I was friendly with when I was at Trinity who always loved to cook. After I got married she sent me a notebook with some of her favourite recipes."

"What sort of things do you like to cook?" asked Eilish.

"This may not come as a surprise, but I can do a few nice French dishes."

"Lovely," said Eilish.

"Do any of those recipes involve boiling lobsters?" asked Mick.

"Just the one," said Sophia.

"So what is your trick for cooking them up? Name them after arrogant surgeons? Or difficult patients?"

"Like anything else, if it has to be done, I just grit my teeth and get on with it."

The cake was a delight of vanilla essence and strawberry jam and everyone's plates were soon clear. There was almost a collective sigh of satisfaction as the last fork rattled onto the last plate.

Sophia broke the silence. "Well, I suppose I'd better be going," she said.

"Sure the night is still young," said Gerry. "Would you like another wee brandy?"

"I'd best not," said Sophia, "otherwise I may end up lost in these hills forever."

"Sure there are worse places to be lost," said Gerry.

"And better, I imagine," said Mick. "This is hardly Tuscany."

"Sure what would you know about Tuscany?" asked Joe.

"I read books," said Mick.

"Now, now, lads," said Sophia. "I'm sure South Armagh has its own particular allures to tempt the traveller, but I must be off. I am on call tomorrow for my practice, so I can't be out carousing no matter how charming the company."

Sophia stood up from the table. "Thanks so much for dinner. It was wonderful."

"It was a lovely evening," said Eilish, amidst the scraping of chairs as everyone else pushed themselves to their feet.

"'Twas," said Gerry.

"Well, maybe next time I can return the compliment. It would be a nice excuse to dig out my recipe for coq au vin."

They all strolled outside. The night was clear and warm, lit silvery by a moon that was approaching its fullest. Below them, on the Dublin Road, they could see the lights of the border check points that Partition had brought this place.

"You know where you are going?" asked Gerry.

"I think so," said Sophia. "If I turn left at the gate and then left again that will bring me back onto the Dublin Road and then I just turn right into Newry."

"That would work, or if you prefer you can turn right at the gate and then right again and the next left will take you straight onto the Dublin Road. It's bit less of a twisty road, so it maybe a wee bit quicker at this time of night."

"I think I will do that, so," said Sophia.

She climbed back into her car and started the engine. "Thanks again," said Sophia out of the window.

"No, thank you," said Gerry, "for bringing Mick home."

"Not a bother," said Sophia.

"No, Sophia. It was a bother," said Mick. "A hundred thousand thanks."

Sophia smiled at Mick then. "I'll be seeing you."

"Don't be a stranger," said Eilish as Sophia turned her car towards the road.

Gerry moved towards Eilish and placed his hand on her shoulder as the four of them stood and watched until the rear lights of the car were swallowed by the night.

Part Three: Mick

XIII

Someone once told me that the nightmares that accompanied killing would eventually fade. But in those days following my release from jail I found that they were back with a vengeance. I dreamt again of the first time I had killed a man, but the face that I saw before my bullet tore a lump from his head was Anthony McCreevy's.

Saturday 23 May 1925

XIV

Over the next week, life settled back into a degree of normalcy. I returned to work, shovelling the cow shite in the slaughterhouse, and reading *Don Quixote* in the evening, though I tended not to go out to secure a pint with it. My mother would get vexed any time I was leaving the house, her imagination working on overtime to conjure the worst that could happen into a certainty, and herself the Cassandra whose perfect foresight was never appreciated. I hoped that her worries would fade with time, but I felt rotten that I had caused her so much stress.

This morning I found myself in the place where it started, back in the Shelbourne, waiting to meet Sophia, "the nice doctor," as my mother called her. She'd become smitten with her when Sophia had delivered me home the previous Friday evening and had stayed for her tea. It seemed that my mother was prepared to let me out of her sight comforted by the knowledge that I was meeting "the nice doctor" who would keep me out of bother just as she had rescued me the previous week.

I didn't want to cause my mother further worry by suggesting to her that Sophia had been the start of my most recent troubles if not really their cause. But I had to say something in mild protest against the beatification of the venerable Sophia.

"You know Queen Elizabeth was a redhead too?" I asked my mother as I slung my arse onto my bicycle saddle.

"Well, so was Mary Magdalen and she turned out okay."

Joe also seemed to have become enamoured with Sophia. When I had mentioned to him that morning that I was going into town to meet Sophia he decided to share a joke.

"Did you hear the one about that Casanova fella, up in front of the Inquisition or something," Joe asked, "being interrogated about his amorous exploits. The Dominican priest questioning him asks, 'Did you ever sleep with blondes?' 'I did,' says Casanova. 'What about brunettes?' 'Them too,' says Casanova. 'What about black-haired women?' asks the Dominican. 'Did you ever sleep with them?' 'Plenty,' says Casanova. 'What about red-heads?' asks the Dominican. 'Did you ever sleep with the gingers?' 'Not a wink.'"

"That," I said to Joe, "is another minute of my life that I am not getting back." But I could still see his point.

Sophia arrived, a breathless bundle of elegant clothes and French perfume. "So sorry I'm late, Mick. There was a roadblock by the B-Specials so I walked to avoid them. I'm afraid I miscalculated a little how long it would take." The B-Specials were a wholly Protestant auxiliary police force, notable for their extreme sectarianism and routine heavy-handedness.

"No worries," I said. "The B-men do like to be extra arseholish on market day, make sure the peasantry know our place. What are you having?"

"Coffee, I think."

I gave a wave to the waitress. She was a pretty girl of about eighteen with bright blue eyes and curly black hair sensibly bound back for work. I presumed she was a daughter of the owners, but was too shy to ask, even though she had been very chatty when I first sat down. She had been very interested in *Don Quixote*. Spain, she reckoned sounded like it had better weather and fewer Protestants than Northern Ireland. Maybe she should go one day.

"Do you speak Spanish," I asked.

"Maybe if I just do like the English and shout at the locals, that will make them understand."

"I'm not sure that works as well as the English think it does."

"Well, I speak a bit of Latin. That might get me started."

"It might," I conceded.

"So what is your book about?"

"You know I'm not sure yet. But it's very funny."

"Well, that is something to be going on with," she said.

She returned to the table now. "Could we have two more coffees please?" I asked. I'd finished my first already while waiting for Sophia.

"And if you had any fruitcake I'd take a piece too," Sophia added. "I had an early house call this morning, so I didn't manage breakfast."

The waitress smiled, all good nature and dimples—I always liked the dimples—and made her way towards the kitchen to prepare our order.

"She likes you," Sophia said once the girl was out of earshot.

"Don't talk rubbish," I said. "She was only being polite."

"Jesus, Mick. She wasn't just being polite. But you have to do a bit of work. It's not like the fairy stories where the boy and the girl just fall into each other's arms."

"I think the moral of many of the fairy stories is that women are nothing but work."

"Why do you say that?"

"Well, imagine ending up with a woman who complains about having a pea left under her mattress. God, if that upset her, what would she be like if you actually did something bad, like forget her birthday, or… you know… accidentally eat her granny?"

"You don't look like a werewolf to me."

"What do werewolves look like?"

"They have one eyebrow."

"Left or right?"

"Both," she said and tapped the space above the bridge of her nose.

"Where did you hear tell of that?"

"Medical school. I am a doctor."

"Not in any of the lectures, though."

"Maybe the end of one once, around the end of some October."

"Hmm," I said. "Well, I'm just saying. I'm sure I would upset a woman in other ways once she got to know me."

"There are some delights known only to the brave."

"I think I am getting too old to be brave."

"Mick, Mick, Mick. You need to be reading *Les Liaisons Dangereuses* instead of *Don Quixote*."

"Ach, I know all about that. You Dubs and your dirty books!"

"It's an indictment of aristocratic corruption."

"You tell yourself that if you need to."

The waitress arrived back with our coffees and cake. She did give me a very nice smile as she left which did leave me wondering if maybe Sophia had half a point.

"See!" she said when the girl had gone.

"See what? There wouldn't be many came back, no matter how nice the coffee is, if she was serving it to you with a face like a slapped arse."

"There's being polite and then there is what that is, which is charm that girl has turned on just for you."

"For God's sake!" I said. "If she had the slightest notion of the things I have been up to these past five years any interest that she might have would evaporate pretty fast."

"I'm not so sure about that, Mick. There is some precedent for women liking the proven warrior. It's how Othello ends up with Desdemona."

"And didn't that love story turn out so well."

"Yes, I suppose that was not the best example."

"Antony and Cleopatra?"

"I see your point."

"Richard the Third and Lady Anne? Brutus and Cassius?"

"You know Shakespeare wrote some comedies too?"

"Like A Midsummer Night's Dream?"

"Yes! Like A Midsummer Night's Dream."

"You know that starts with the wedding of Theseus and Hippolyta, the queen of the Amazons?"

"I do and the play worked out pretty well for everyone."

"Except for Hippolyta. Theseus murders her after the end of the play."

"Jesus! Why?"

"Well, knowing Theseus' proclivities, I presume she was getting in the way of him raping more children."

Sophia took a drink of her coffee. "Jesus," she said again, "for you, Mick, the joys of spring are just things that happen to other people."

"Aye. Sure I wouldn't want to inflict that on anyone else."

"Maybe someone else is the cure that you're needing."

"Let me ruminate on that," I said. "Meantime, have you heard anything back from Sparky?"

"You mean Martin Crosby?"

"I do."

"Why Sparky?"

"Don't know. It just seemed to fit."

"Didn't he save your life once?"

"Aye, he did."

"Well, maybe be a bit more respectful then."

I had forgotten she could be fierce in her loyalties. I sipped my coffee. "Didn't mean to be rude," I said. "It was more affectionate teasing."

"Hmm."

"So, did you hear anything from him?"

"Not yet," she said. "Have the police been near you about Anthony again."

"No, thankfully."

"Poor young fella. He was buried last week, I hear. Did you go to the funeral?"

"I didn't think it was a good idea. I think his Ma saw us talking and some suspicion may linger with her."

"Do you have any thoughts on who might have killed him?"

"To start with I was wondering why he might have been killed."

"What do you think?"

I leaned towards her so I could whisper.

"Are you sure it really was Anthony was the father of Collette's baby?"

"It's what she told me."

"When I spoke to him he was pretty adamant to the contrary."

"That doesn't mean that he wasn't."

"Well, let's think this through for a minute: suppose Collete's Da heard that Anthony was the father of his daughter's child, is that really motive for murder?"

"Some fathers can get wild cranky about the sexual virtue of their daughters."

"I remember you saying. But your Da didn't round up a couple of his pals and put your Charlie in the nearest bog, did he."

"Not really the sort of my father... but hold on. What do you mean a couple of his pals?"

"I don't think that sort of killing is really a one-man job."

"How do you know that?"

I said nothing, and let Sophia do the realising on her own.

"Okay," she said slowly, drawing herself back to the now. "But I think we have established that Hoey is a bad bastard, perhaps with comparable experiences to yourself, Mick. I don't think we can rule out that he doesn't go homicidally berserk with the least provocation."

"True enough. But if he heard Anthony was the daddy, mightn't he get the shotgun out rather than the Webley?"

"You mean force him to marry Collette?"

"I do."

"Hmm—maybe before he'd packed Collette off to the nunnery. Maybe once she'd gone Anthony was just a loose end?"

"Maybe," I said. "But I can't help feeling that Anthony's death had something to do with us poking around, specifically with me speaking to him."

"But how can that be?"

"Anthony did intimate to me that Collette may have talked to him about more than school work. He actually talked about not breaking her confidences to a stranger like me."

"So?" Sophia asked.

"So suppose Collette did confide in Anthony that she was pregnant, maybe even hinting at who the father was. Suppose then, with me coming round and suggesting that maybe Anthony was the baby's father, that that is what spooked him: the idea of being unjustly accused."

"Suppose indeed. But how does that get him from being upset to being dead in a field."

"Let's think about it another way. You've probably read more Freud and Jung than I have. Isn't most sexual assault perpetrated by someone known to the victim?"

"Perhaps... outside of wartime," she said and took a sip of her coffee.

"And isn't much sexual abuse perpetrated inside the family?"

Sophia set down her cup. "Her own father?"

"Hadn't that crossed your mind already?"

"It was an initial thought when she first came to see me, particularly when I saw her distress. But then she told me a tale of love's young dream."

"Well, if Anthony was not the father, but knew or suspected who was, might he have thought he should do something about it?"

"You mean confront Hoey? Sure that would be suicide and from what you have said, Anthony did not sound like an eejit."

"Maybe not. But wanting to cover up an accusation of incest would be a pretty powerful motive for murder, don't you think? There's one thing knowing yourself the sort of person you are. There's another having others know about it. Never understood it myself but some seem to regard the spreading of so-called 'scandal' as worse than the thing itself."

"Vices are fine so long as you're discreet?"

"Aye, that sort of thing."

"You said that Anthony's killing was not a one man job. How do you think Hoey could have gotten others to do his bidding? I mean I can't think it would be easy to stir up much of a hue and cry to kill a young fella at the best of times."

I took a sip of my coffee. "The accusation of being an informer is a powerful thing. I imagine there are some morons in our revolutionary brotherhood who would happily cart off a mother of ten and put a bullet in her if the right person whispered that she might be a tout."

Sophia said nothing and took a mouthful of her coffee. "So where does this leave us. Should I speak to your good friend Inspector Hanby, and tell him of our suspicions?"

"Sophia, if Anthony could end up dead in a ditch on a false accusation of being an informer, what do you think could happen to you with a genuine accusation?"

"We can't just keep our mouths shut?"

"Oh I think we can."

"You've changed."

"Bleeding right I have changed. I know what it's like to be in prison, and I know what it's like to be in the police barracks in Newry and I have no desire to be in either ever again."

"Oh Mick."

"Look, who would listen to us anyway? All we have is theory and supposition. And Hoey is living in the Free State where Hanby has no jurisdiction."

"I do know someone who has though."

"Who?"

"Your old buddy, Eamon Gleason. Or as I should now more properly say, Detective Inspector Eamon Gleason of *An Garda Siochana.*"

XV

So that is why, the next Saturday I found myself sitting amongst the rattle of cups and the chatter of the clientele with Sophia in Bewley's coffee house in Dublin waiting for Eamon.

"This must be like Shangri-La for you?" I said inhaling the aroma of the coffee that enveloped the place.

"It's not Milan, Mick, but it's maybe as good as it gets on the island of Ireland."

"Have you been to Milan?"

"Just once, a long time ago."

"One day, if I can ever save enough money, I'd like to do one of them Grand Tours, through France and Italy, see some of the art I've only ever read about. What was your favourite thing in Milan."

"I really liked that painting of Mary Magdalene having her tea with Jesus."

I looked at Sophia, somewhat bemused. "That's a picture I have never heard of."

"What? You have never heard of Leonardo da Vinci's Last Supper?"

"Mary Magdalene is not in the Last Supper."

"Well, who is that ginger sitting beside Jesus then?"

"I've only seen a black and white photograph. But I thought that it was St John was meant to be sitting beside Jesus."

"So, who was it made them their dinner then? Sure, if Mary Magdalene was not with them all the time they would have all starved."

"Well, maybe she was in the kitchen when Leonardo made the initial sketch?"

"Jesus, Mick, you really have a lot to learn about women."

"I did not know this was something you felt so passionately about."

"Well, I have to stick up for my people."

"The gingers?"

"Gingers in general. Red-headed women in particular."

"Even Queen Elizabeth."

"Now you're just being silly."

I laughed at that and looked at my watch. "Eamon's running a bit late," I said.

"He's busy and important. But I'm sure he'll be here soon enough."

It was Sophia who had organised the meeting. I had not seen Eamon since I joined the flying column in 1920. However, Sophia had lived in the same village in Mayo as him until 1922. He had commanded the local battalion of the IRA until the Truce, when he had taken himself off to Dublin to join the Guards. But she also knew, she told me, from Eamon's mother in Mayo, who she still corresponded with occasionally, what station he was assigned to in Dublin. So, having made a few phone calls, she had managed to speak to him this past Wednesday.

Eamon was working Saturday, a day that both of us had off. But he said he could meet us for an hour or so at lunchtime, and Sophia, always on the lookout for good coffee, had suggested Bewleys.

"So where else have you been to in Italy?"

"Just the usual tourist spots. Florence, Rome, Venice."

"So: favourite bits?"

"Venice is stunning, but the canals are a bit manky. I had a very expensive cup of coffee there, in St Mark's Square, but they did have a string quartet playing Vivaldi as well."

"Is that why you came to Newry: with the nice coffee and the manky canal it must be like the Venice of Ireland."

"Yes. It's exactly like the Venice of Ireland."

"And what was Rome like?"

"Probably just what you imagine. Walk down one street and, all of a sudden, there is the Trevi Fountain. Walk down another and there is the Colosseum."

"No lions any more though."

"The poor Christians were lucky if there were lions. A lot of the time they threw them to dogs, pit bulls and the like."

"Jesus."

"I know. Horrible to think about. But for such an awful cruel crowd of bastards two thousand years ago they are properly lovely now."

"Gives us some hope for ourselves."

"Steady!"

"Did you see the Pope?"

"No. But we did go to the Vatican. Had a wander round St Peter's, had a look at the Sistine Chapel and the Vatican Museum."

"The Sistine Chapel. That's the one that Michelangelo painted the ceiling?"

"It is. It took him five years?"

"Jesus. He can't have been much of a painter so. I know fellas could have had that done in a week."

"That is a truly dreadful joke, Mick," said Sophia.

"You win some, you lose some," I said.

"It is breath-taking though. Worth every minute he spent on it."

"Ah, someday I'll get there," I said.

"Definitely, you should."

"Who did you go to Italy with? Your parents?"

"No. I went with Charlie. It was our honeymoon."

"It sounds just lovely."

"It was. When we were young and both thought the world was full of promise, not the awful bastard it has turned out to be."

I drank some of my coffee as I ruminated upon that.

"There he is now!" Sophia jumped up and waved as I twisted round to see. And there he was. Older than the last time I saw him, and more neatly turned out, clean-shaven in a dark suit and tie, but still looking lean and fit. He waved back and wove his way through the tables towards us.

"Jaysus! Look at the two of ye!" he said. He folded me into a bear hug and slapped my back. "Good to see you Mick." Sophia, he greeted with a kiss on each cheek. "*Tres Parisian*," I thought.

"Who broke your nose, Mick?" Eamon asked as we sat down.

"The peelers."

"The RUC you mean?"

"Aye."

"Fuckers! Well, it looks good on you."

"So," he said as he settled himself, "what's the craic?"

"Still alive," Sophia said. "You've been prospering I hear."

"Ach, I've been doing okay. But the life of a policeman is hardly a glamorous one."

"Detective inspector though. Still a leader of men," Sophia said. "It's not like you have to clean up the drunks on a Saturday night."

Eamon let out a chuckle. "That's true. But dealing with bank robbers can be a bit nerve wracking given the number of guns that are still lying about, and murder is always a sad thing."

A waitress glided towards our table. "Can I get you anything?" she asked.

"Coffee would be good, please," said Eamon.

"I'd take another one too," I said. I was down to the dregs.

"Me too," said Sophia.

The girl seemed to hesitate. "Em... do you mean filter coffee, cappuccino, café au lait, or espresso?"

"What we had before," I said.

"Sorry I did not take your order before," she said. It was Sophia who had ordered when I was in the bathroom.

"Cappuccinos please," said Sophia, "unless you'd prefer something different, Eamon?"

"No, cappuccino would suit me just fine," said Eamon.

"So three cappuccinos please," said Sophia by way of confirmation.

"Grand," said the girl, and set off. I watched her thread her way amongst the tables, balancing her tray on one hand with the elegance of a ballet dancer, back towards the kitchen. Then I turned back towards Eamon.

"So, any woman on the go?" I asked.

"Too busy with work," Eamon said.

Sophia snorted. "The two of you are as bad as each other. Face down the armies of the British and German empires at the drop of a hat, but terrified by the sight of a small brunette with affectionate intent."

"I suppose I've been spoiled for other women. I've yet to meet anyone who comes to the same standard as my wife." Eamon had been married to a French nurse who had been killed during the Great War.

"You need to move on, Eamon," said Sophia. "You're still a young man... well... relatively young anyway. Juliette would not want you to be alone."

"Maybe," said Eamon. "But what about ye? I know you're both in Newry now. What are you up to, Mick? Back to the law."

Sophia snorted again.

"I'm shovelling shite in an abattoir," I said.

"Just for the summer though?" asked Eamon.

"I'm afraid the dream of a legal career died in jail. Don't have the cash to pay for it even if any university would accept me."

"Jesus," said Eamon, "that's a crying shame."

"Isn't it," said Sophia. "But he won't listen to me. Maybe you can talk some sense into him."

"I'd heard you got lifted when you went home, Mick. So you spent the Civil War in jail?"

"I did. On the prison ship Argenta in Belfast Lough."

"That can't have been nice."

"It wasn't. But it was an education of sorts I suppose."

"I'm sorry about that, Mick. But never underestimate the worse luck that your bad luck may have saved you from."

"I suppose it saved me from maybe being asked to turn my gun on neighbours or former comrades," I said.

"I suppose it also saved other neighbours and former comrades from turning their guns on you," said Sophia.

"That too," I said, "but it was hardly a non-violent environment. The screws were not at all sympathetic to the nationalist cause."

"I can only imagine," said Eamon. "But you survived. That's the important thing."

"That's what I told him too," said Sophia.

The waitress arrived back with our coffees and dealt them out to us, and retrieved our dirty cups.

"Would youse like a bit of chocolate on the top?" she asked, proffering what looked like a shiny metal can towards us.

The words, "What witchcraft is this?" went through my mind, but when Sophia and Eamon said yes and offered their cups towards her for what turned out to be a dusting with chocolate powder, I thought I should probably agree to it too for fear of appearing the bumpkin.

We offered a chorus of thank-yous as she departed us.

"What about you then?" Eamon asked Sophia.

"Same story, different place," she said, "mostly mothers, children and the elderly. The routine of general practice. But my partners are sound, and working with nice people is always important."

"What brought you North? Didn't like the notion of living under Rome-rule in the South?"

"Go away and shite," said Sophia. "There is only one Ireland, and I moved to a different part of it. It was a good work opportunity and I needed a change of scene. Anyway, there is a good chance that Newry and South Armagh will soon be part of the Free State with the deliberations of the Boundary Commission. You think the Northern Ireland Government is going to want to retain such a hostile portion of its territory?"

"The only thing I know about Newry," said Eamon, "apart from what Mick told me, is that doggerel from Jonathan Swift."

I knew the rhyme. "*High church with a low steeple, dirty streets and a proud people.*"

"That about sums it up," said Sophia.

"You just called it the Venice of Ireland, before Eamon arrived."

"I did," conceded Sophia.

"I thought Cork was the Venice of Ireland," said Eamon.

"Cork has always got notions of itself," I said.

"It is lovely though," said Sophia.

"It is," said Eamon.

"I've not been there," I said, "but I have met a lot of Cork folk."

"I suppose that would put you off agreeing with them," said Eamon.

"Why?" asked Sophia. "Were they particularly horrible?"

"Not at all," I said, "but they do go on about it as if it's the centre of the universe."

"I thought Derry was the centre of the universe," said Sophia.

"Exactly," I said. "Cork is the Derry of the South! The rest of us should not be encouraging their notions of themselves."

"Derry too?" asked Sophia.

"Yes. Not least for them unloading John Mitchel onto Newry."

"Jail Journal John Mitchel?" asked Eamon.

"The very one," I said.

"But he I thought he was a hero of nationalist Ireland," said Sophia.

"Aye, and of Confederate America too," I said. "The fucker not only thought slavery was okay but wanted to reinstitute the trans-Atlantic slave trade. His notion of an independent Ireland was one in which we could be as big a bunch of bastards to the rest of the world as the English."

"Could he not be excused a bit as being a man of his times?" asked Eamon.

"Daniel O'Connell was a man of the same times. So was Frederick Douglass. They were pretty clear-sighted about what was right and wrong when it came to slavery. Mitchel's attitude makes him a disgrace to our country."

"So why is this Derry's fault?" asked Sophia.

"He came from County Derry. But somehow he is now forever associated with Newry."

"Because that is where he is buried?" asked Sophia.

"That and, I suppose, because it's where he grew up too," I said.

"So Newry bears some responsibility for him," said Eamon.

"You could look at it that way, I suppose," I said. "But I would prefer to blame him completely on Derry."

"And Newry is the Venice of Ireland," said Eamon, circling back.

"Now you have it," I said. "Greenish canals, good coffee and the Protestant end of the town is well posh," I said.

"It is," said Sophia, "and in Mitchel we have a former resident who was as big a bastard as some of the Doges."

"You are sounding very pro-Newry all of a sudden, Mick," Eamon said. "Why so? You were the one who told me about the 'Newry *Nyeuks*' and always made a big deal of being from South Armagh, not Newry."

It was a good point. "Well, I've made some more friends there since I got out of jail. I suppose I've come to appreciate it a bit more."

"Loyalty," said Eamon, "often an admirable quality."

We drank some coffee and Eamon and Sophia lit up.

"How did you spend the Civil War?" I asked Eamon as he extinguished a match and blew a cloud of smoke towards the ceiling.

"I joined the Guards on their formation in 1922. We've been mostly unarmed since 1923."

"So you avoided the fighting altogether."

"Not quite. There were a few bank jobs where the lines blurred, some of them by freelancers from both sides, some of them official anti-treaty operations. And some of the more rabid of the anti-treaty partisans regarded any functionary of the Free State as fair game."

"Did that include you?"

"Someone took a couple of pot shots at me once, but they couldn't have hit the side of a barn if they tried. Probably a 'trucileer', who joined up after the fighting with the British was done. No real idea of what it takes to kill a man."

"What happened to him?"

"No idea. Like the vermin he was, he skedaddled faster than a rat up a drainpipe. So I never saw hide nor hair of him after that."

"Lucky for you both I suppose. You avoided killing him and he avoided getting killed," I said.

"I tell myself that too. But, truth be told, I do take it personally when someone tries to kill me So I would really like to have plugged that little bastard."

"So you avoided the killing altogether?" asked Sophia.

"That's a more difficult question. Some of the folk I arrested ended up facing the death penalty."

"How do you feel about that?" I asked.

"Not great. But sentencing is for the courts to decide not me. Though if anyone asks my opinion I'll tell them. I have enough blood on my hands not to want any more."

"Still, you survived and prospered," Sophia said.

"I suppose I did," said Eamon.

"Good for you," I said. "The way that Orange government in Belfast treats us, we don't have your sort of options. We're just like them Untouchable fellas out in India."

Eamon leaned back in the chair. "Your erudition never fails to impress me Mick. Where did you hear about the Untouchables?"

"In jail. There was a fella there had been a merchant seaman, had sailed the world."

"That makes sense. I met a couple of Indian fellas in France during the war, who told me about the Untouchables."

"So you know what I'm talking about then."

"Ach I wouldn't claim that, Mick. I've not been to the North since Partition. I only have the newspapers to go on. So I never really appreciated the depth of discrimination you have to put up with."

"Aye."

"So how do you get your water?"

"What do you mean?"

"Well, you know that some fuckers don't allow Untouchables to use the community water sources because it's believed they make them ritually impure. So they have to walk hours out of their way to get water and sometimes have to share the same wells with the livestock."

"Well, we still have the town water supply in Newry. And there is a well at my parent's house."

"Oh that's a relief. But I suppose it's fair."

"What do you mean fair?"

"Well, if your conditions are like the Untouchables then you must be forced to clean the shite out of the Protestant sewers and outhouses for a living. It would be terrible if you couldn't wash after."

"I'm working in the abattoir."

"So you have some choice in your work?"

"Well, it's not really my first choice, but at least its only cow shite I'm shovelling."

"Still, it must put you off starting a family."

"What the fuck has that got to do with anything?"

"Well, if you're just like the Untouchables you know you'll have to hand over your first born child on their second birthday to be a slave for the master in the big house."

"Em... I don't think it has quite come to that yet."

Eamon looked at me. "You're not really at the same level of discrimination as the Untouchables yet so."

"Smug fucker," I said.

"Come on now, Mick. I'm not pretending that there are not problems or that there is not discrimination. But there's many have it way worse than you. Particularly a man with your brains and education. It's far easier for the oppressor to keep you down if you agree with him that's where you should be."

"Exactly," said Sophia.

"I thought we were here to talk about Collette Hoey, not for the two of you to gang up on me with life advice."

"Well," said Sophia, "I am a woman, so used to doing several things at once."

"Who's this Collette Hoey?" Eamon asked.

Sophia began to recount our travails over the previous weeks, with me chipping in my encounters with Hanby, and our theories about Collette's father and Anthony's killing.

"So Hoey actually threatened to kill you if you came around again?" Eamon asked when we had finished.

"He did," Sophia said.

"And he was serious too," I added. "I've seen that look on fuckers before."

"That does rather suggest he's feeling guilty about something," said Eamon.

"But I don't suppose it counts as evidence," said Sophia.

"No, and this does pose something of an investigative dilemma. Hoey is living in the Free State, but young Anthony is from Northern Ireland where he was presumably killed and definitely found."

"That is the gist of it."

"And you think Hoey might be the culprit because Anthony bad-mouthed him as an incestuous rapist."

"It's a theory."

"So things rather hinge on what Collette has to say about that doesn't it?"

"It does," I said.

115

"So, what about Collette? Any word from his Eminence about her?"

"He's tracked her down to a Mother and Baby home in Castleblayney," said Sophia.

"Also in the Free State then."

"Yes."

"Well, ye are doing well as detectives, veritable Poirots, the two of ye!"

"Who?" I asked.

"Hercule Poirot," Eamon said. "You haven't read any Agatha Christie?"

"I've been in jail."

"Well, something for you to look forward to then," he said and took a mouthful of coffee. "Poirot is Christie's genius detective protagonist."

"Sort of like Holmes but Belgian," said Sophia.

"So, a bit of a prick but prefers chocolate to cocaine?" I asked.

"A lot of a prick… but yes," said Sophia.

"So, you're calling us pricks, Eamon?" I asked, in mock offence.

"Jaysus!" said Eamon, laughing, "that went very quickly in a direction I wasn't expecting. I was saying you've done some good detective work that even a prick like Poirot could be proud of."

"Kind of you to say, Eamon. But that is hardly the case," I said. "Not least because we have no authority to ask people questions that they do not want to answer."

"So what do you want from me then?" Eamon asked.

"Well, first of all, that big detective brain of yours that your mother was always telling me about," said Sophia.

"You've begun believing Irishmen's mothers about their sons now, Sophia? Are you really keeping well? Not been kicked in the head by a horse or something."

"I think your Ma is a hard-headed enough, woman, Eamon, even accounting for the favourable prejudice that she has towards you."

Eamon snorted. "Well, the first thing, I think, would be to get Collette's story on record, to see if your supposition has any reality in fact. As well as the information on Collette's whereabouts, did Crosby provide you with anything useful, like a papal bull, or failing that, at least a letter of introduction to the nuns in question?"

"He did send me that. Do you want to see it?"

"Not right now thanks, Sophia. I'll have a look at it later."

"So, what next then," I asked.

"Feck it," said Eamon. "I do have a day off on Wednesday."

"Are you saying you would be willing to come northwards and help us poke around a bit, see how Collette's doing?" I asked.

"You know I went to the Christian Brothers school, don't you?"

"I do," said Sophia.

"Aye," I said.

"Well, I had a religion teacher for a couple of years called Sister Delores. She was a nasty old woman, just loved to bully and beat young fellas. I presume the reason she was in the Christian Brothers' school was that she was deemed too vicious for the girls."

"It hardened you so?" I asked.

"No," Eamon said. "It just made a couple of years miserable."

"So what's that got to do with anything?" Sophia asked.

"I think that there's some nuns are overdue for a bit of retaliation for Sister Dolores."

XVI

After Eamon left us to return to his duties, Sophia suggested going to the national art gallery for a bit of a treat before catching our train home. "It's not the Louvre," she said, "but it would be a taster for your Grand Tour."

We walked together up onto St Stephen's Green pausing to observe the bullet holes from the rebellion on the façade of the College of Surgeons.

"Did you hear tell the story that the Countess Markiewicz personally shot an unarmed police man here during the rising?" Sophia asked.

"I did," I said. "I think there was very bad blood between her lot, the Citizen's Army, and the Dublin police going back to the Lockout in 1913." The Citizen's Army had been drawn entirely from the trade union movement.

"Still," she said, "that does seem harsh."

"*When the weapons are out, the laws tend to fall silent,*" I said.

"Wrong is still wrong."

"It is," I said.

We crossed the Green and made our way towards the gallery. "Anything in particular you would recommend me to see?" I asked her in the entry hall.

"I was reading that they have acquired some of Jack Yeats' new paintings."

"Any relation to WB?"

"A brother, I think."

"Talented bastards!" I said.

She laughed. "And they have some Degas too, which you should like."

"Why should I like them?"

"Well, he's French."

"So?" I asked.

"Dancers and naked girls," she said.

I realised that I was, of all things at this stage in my life, blushing and Sophia saw it. "I said it before," she said, "you should read *Les Liaisons Dangereuses*, understand a bit more of our common European culture."

"I've read *The Rights of Man*, you know," I said. "That's a French book!"

"But not *A Vindication of the Rights of Women*, I imagine."

"No," I admitted.

"Ach, there is still hope for you, Mick."

We wandered around the gallery for about an hour, occasionally together, occasionally apart. The Yeats' paintings I did find particularly arresting. Another by Sean Keating, Men of the South made me catch my breath. The title card stated that it was on loan from the Crawford Gallery in Cork, so I was lucky to see it. A study of a small group of armed men, part, it seemed to me, of an IRA unit in the field. It reminded me of those days, years ago in the West, constantly afraid, or tired or both, when I was part of the flying column, hoping that what we were doing would lead to a better future for all the people of our country. Now, however, I was beginning finally to appreciate more the other Yeats' assessment of those years: "*The blood-dimmed tide is loosed, and everywhere the ceremony of innocence is drowned.*"

Looking back across those years I barely recognised the naive person I had been before I had to flee Galway ahead of the police, ending up finally in the West Mayo Flying Column and then jail on the Argenta.

Sophia was right too. I did love the Degas. Hard as I looked, there were no nudes that I could find. But I loved his paintings of dancers. It was extraordinary, I thought, how such small images, capturing such brief moments in these girls' lives, could convey so completely the sense of effort and exhaustion that was fundamental to their work.

At the end we rendezvoused at the entrance to the gallery. We had about forty-five minutes before our train so we decided to walk in the direction of the station. We could, we agreed, always get a drink in the bar of the station hotel if we arrived early, which we did.

It was a genteel affair with white table clothes and a few middle-aged couples sitting around sipping sherry, also waiting for their trains. I bought a pint of porter for myself and a glass of red wine for Sophia and brought them to the table that she had secured for us.

"When were you last in Dublin?" asked Sophia as she sipped her wine.

"God, ages ago. Almost ten years. Before the Rising. I was initially thinking of studying in Dublin and had got as far as visiting some of the universities here?"

"You were almost a Trinity man then?"

"I think my mother would have had a conniption if I had gone to a Protestant bastion like Trinity."

"I can understand that. Sure that's way worse than shooting people you have never met as a member of a flying column."

I smiled. "Aye, I've given her some grey hairs, there's no doubt about that."

"I can imagine her giving thanks every day once you were safely locked up in jail for a bit."

"You seem to know my mother so well. What were youse talking about when I wasn't there," I asked.

"Nothing too earth shattering," said Sophia. "Just small talk."

"I suppose it is the role and curse of mothers to worry."

"Not just mothers."

"I suppose. But I don't really have anyone else to be fretting over me, for which I am eternally thankful."

"You're an awful fucking eejit sometimes, Mick." That took me aback a bit, but I was getting used to her being blunt.

"I certainly have been, but I thought I was getting better."

"Well, you are not fully cured yet," she said.

"For example?"

"You don't think your Da and your brother worry sick about you too? You don't think that there are other people who care about you? Maybe they don't say it as explicitly as your mother, but they must have been eaten away by fear these past couple of years. Not just about what might happen to you, but what you might do, what you might become in the midst of all that carnage."

I was saved from this onslaught by the call for the train. We tried to drink down the remainder of our drinks but failed.

121

"Now I see why the Dutch invented the resealable beer bottle," said Sophia as we abandoned the remainders of our drinks.

We headed to the platform. Sophia had bought us both first class tickets for the journey. There were few others in our carriage so we had plenty of space to settle in. I pulled *Don Quixote* out of my bag. Sophia had something by a bloke called Balzac, in French, of course.

"Another dirty book?" I asked. She laughed and closed it over but kept her page marked with her finger.

"You know," said Sophia, "that talk about Dutch inventions reminded me of something I was thinking about in the gallery."

"What was that?" I asked.

"You know Vincent Van Gogh only sold like one painting in his lifetime, and that was to his own brother."

"I didn't see any Van Gogh when I was in there. Where was it?"

"There wasn't any. I was just thinking."

"About how much they are worth now?"

"Not quite. The poor man went to his grave thinking that he was a failure, and he is now increasingly recognised as one of the greatest artists of his day, perhaps of all time."

"Makes you think," I said.

"Well, I hope so," said Sophia. "Partition. Jail. Your failure to get a degree. Your presumption that outside of your family there is no one that cares about you. You are at risk of becoming a man who has decided his life is a failure and so decides to make it so."

"That is easy to say if you are a person who has not had your opportunities snatched away."

"Everyone gets knocked down, Mick. It's the getting up again that is the charm."

"Maybe, but the world is hardly missing a genius of Van Gogh's proportions with me failing to get a law degree."

"How do we know unless you put the hard work in. That is what Van Gogh did and look at what riches the world has as a result. It's time for you to spill sweat for Ireland, not more blood."

"I'm spilling plenty of sweat for Ireland. Particularly on the hot days. That abattoir gets like an oven."

"You are always with the jokes when the truth gets too close to the bone, Mick."

"Maybe," I said. "But why does it matter to you? Shouldn't you be looking at the log in your own eye before poking at the specks in someone else's?"

"What log are you referring to?" she asked.

"A woman like yourself…" I started but trailed off.

"Go on," she said, "let's hear about a woman like myself."

"A woman like yourself could be doing a lot better than pining after a man that is both unavailable and unworthy of you."

"Really, Mick? You are such an awful fecking eejit." She opened her book and, with an exhalation that brooked no further comment, began to read.

I followed suite and the two of us spent the rest of the journey like that, looking up only to catch the view over Drogheda harbour and the mouth of the Boyne, another place that the fate of the Catholics of Ireland had turned for the worse.

Don Quixote was having an unfortunate encounter with larcenous galley slaves. But, Quixote tells Sancho, "*It is not the responsibility of knights errant to discover whether the afflicted, the enchained and the oppressed whom they encounter on the road are reduced to these circumstances and suffer this distress for their vices or for their virtues: The knight's sole responsibility is to succour them as people in need, having eyes only for their sufferings, not for their misdeeds."*

So, like me it seemed, Don Quixote was also an awful eejit. And he didn't quite understand why either.

Part Four: Sophia and Eamon

Wednesday 3 June 1925

XVII

Sophia picked Eamon up in her car from the early train in Dundalk and drove from there over to Castleblayney. He wore his uniform for the occasion, but carried his old army satchel with a change of shirt inside, in case, he said, he needed to venture into the North.

Mick had been unable to get the day off work so it was just the two of them. Eamon perused the letter of introduction Bishop Crosby had sent as Sophia drove. "This is very good," he said. "Of course, I should have brought my old Webley, just in case the nuns need a bit more convincing."

"I don't think we will be needing that," said Sophia.

"We may not be needing it," said Eamon, "but if we bump into the likes of Sister Dolores again, we may be wanting it."

"Jesus," said Sophia. "Boys and their toys."

"I know," said Eamon. "But we're simple souls really."

They drove on in silence for a bit. "So, you and his Eminence are no longer a thing," Eamon said. Eamon was one of the few people in the world who knew about her affair with Martin, begun after her husband, Charlie, had been killed in France.

"How did you know that?"

"You told me."

"When?"

"Just now."

"Shite," said Sophia. "Give me a cigarette."

Eamon manipulated the end of a cigarette out of the pack and then proffered it so that she could catch it with her lips. He struck a match and lit her up, and then lit another for himself.

"You must think you are so clever," Sophia said.

"I have my moments," said Eamon. "So what's the craic?"

"We've not been a thing for several years now."

"Whose idea was it to end it?"

"It was hardly a practical proposition to continue once he'd been appointed a bishop."

"His then. Selfish fucker."

"We're hardly living in renaissance Italy, are we Eamon? I don't think the Catholic church makes the same provisions for episcopal mistresses as it once did."

"How has that been for you?"

"Not much point complaining about the unavoidable."

"I know what you mean," said Eamon, "but it must be hard. The end of an affair can be like a bereavement."

"It can. I'm sure it's not worse than an actual bereavement, but it's still horrible and has that added pain associated with the fact that the other person is still alive and well and seems to be perfectly happy without you."

"I doubt that Martin is keeping perfectly fine. I imagine he too is tortured by all those fevered memories of passionate embraces and carnal lusts."

Sophia laughed. Eamon's humour had always stretched to the earthy. "I certainly hope so," she said.

"That's the spirit," said Eamon. "Not many people to talk to about it either, given the secrecy. Is that why you sought out Mick? Whatever his skills as a detective, he's someone you could be a bit more candid with than the rest of the hoi polloi."

"He's a good man."

"Aye. He likes you too."

"What do you mean?"

"Jesus, Sophia. Sure you are leading him around like a puppy. He'd hardly be in this thing if it wasn't for you."

"Mick is a grown man. He can make up his own mind."

"That's the sort of thing green-eyed witches have been saying for centuries."

"And that is the sort of thing that men have been saying for millennia when they don't have the guts to take responsibility for their own actions. 'Eve made me do it, Lord. It was her fault not mine!'"

"You may have a point there," said Eamon. "I'm rarely able to resist an apple, whether a woman is offering it to me or not."

"He's been through the mill, has Mick. He just needs to get back on his feet again."

"I know," said Eamon. "He seemed a bit broken, and I don't just mean his nose."

"Bruised, not broken, I think," said Sophia.

They were quiet for a while taking in the views of the blue Ring of Gullion mountains that stretched from here through South Armagh to the edge of Newry.

"Cuchulainn country," said Eamon.

"It is that," Sophia replied. It was in these mountains, legend had it, that, thousands of years ago, the armies of Connaught came off second best when they clashed with the Ulster champion Cuchulainn, as they tried to steal the prized Brown Bull of Cooley.

"Does it make a Connaught man like yourself nervous?" Sophia asked.

"I come in peace this time."

"No Queen Mebh to lead the poor, innocent men astray."

"Like I told you, Sophia: Men are simple creatures, and Queen Mebh was a green-eyed woman."

Eamon ground out the remains of his cigarette between his fingers and thumb and dropped it out of the car window. "When you think about it," said Eamon, "Cuchulainn must have been a nightmare to be around. You'd never know when he'd go off on one of his berserker sprees, harvesting up the heads of his enemies as if they were apples. Sort of fella that would take your own head clean off too if he had too many scoops and you said the wrong thing to him."

"I know," said Sophia. "A lot of them 'heroes', all the way back to Heracles, would have killed you as soon as look at you."

"That's maybe why the bards wrote such nice poems about them: not from admiration but from fear."

"That's just wrong. It's the warriors should be afraid of the poets not the other way around."

"In a just world, maybe," said Eamon. "But you know what they say. In poker, a Colt forty-five beats a royal flush every time."

Sophia smiled. But she was not feeling happy. Instead she was aware of a deep sense of foreboding growing in the pit of her stomach, worrying now that she was close to finding Collette she would not be able to help her much.

"I know you must be an experienced interrogator, Eamon. But can I take the lead on talking to Collette? She may not even like you being in the room given some of the questions we have for her."

"You are right," said Eamon. "But ideally I should be there, so I can record her account. If we can get to see her at all, of course."

"For now, let's just hope for the best."

Eventually Castleblayney hove into view and she negotiated the streets to the address that Crosby had sent her. Even in the summer sun the Mother and Child home had a chilling aspect. Behind its grey walls it looked more like a prison than a hospital. She parked across the street from it.

"Well, hopefully Martin's letter will do the trick. But if that doesn't work then maybe you can play the police card."

"And if that doesn't work we can always come back and try the Webley?" asked Eamon.

"Jaysus," said Sophia. "Enough with your fecking Webleys!" said Sophia.

XVIII

A thin, timid-looking young nun ushered Sophia and Eamon into the Mother Superior's office. She was sitting behind a desk inspecting Crosby's letter which she laid down before her as they entered. She stood up.

"Hello. I am Mother Romana."

The Mother Superior's office was an austere one. It was white walled and had a large crucifix over the currently unlit fireplace. Sophia noted that it had considerably fewer books than Martin's office.

"Good of you to see us, Mother Superior," said Sophia.

"Please be seated," said Mother Romana, gesturing to two wooden chairs before her desk. Sophia and Eamon sat down. Romana resumed her own seat.

"So, what can I do for you?" Mother Romana asked.

"You have read the letter from Bishop Crosby," Sophia asked.

"Belfast is a long way from Castleblayney. The bishop has no authority in this diocese."

"No, but as the bishop said, he would appreciate it as a courtesy if we could speak to Collette Hoey," said Sophia.

"What is this in relation to?" asked Mother Romana.

"As it states in Bishop Crosby's letter, I am Collette's doctor and I have some concerns about her well-being."

"Does that normally require a police escort?" asked Mother Romana.

"Inspector Gleason is an old friend."

"Lovely. But that doesn't answer my question, does it? Why is he here? And why are the two of you here together?"

"Dr Hennessy is helping me with an enquiry," said Eamon.

"Does that enquiry involve Collette Hoey?"

"It does. So we have something of a common interest in speaking with her."

"What can a fourteen year old girl have done to bring her to the attention of so distinguished a personage as a detective inspector?"

"I'm sure you appreciate, Mother Superior, that we are at a sensitive stage in our enquiries."

"I will need more than that," Romana said. "We are here *in loco parentis*. No parent would offer their child to interrogation by the police without more information than that."

Eamon sighed. "A short while ago a youth was found shot dead just over the border in South Armagh. We understand he was known to Collette."

"How short a while ago?"

"Towards the beginning of May."

"Collette came to us at the end of April. I can promise you that she was not wandering the countryside shooting young men in early May."

"We would like to speak to her as a potential witness, not as a suspect."

"I'm afraid that will not be possible," Romana said.

"I can return with a warrant," said Eamon.

"Good luck with that," said Romana. "What Free State court is going to issue a warrant in connection to an investigation in Northern Ireland? And even if that was possible do you think any court in Ireland is going to authorise such an intrusion into a religious establishment?"

Eamon thought he detected a slight smirk hovering on Romana's otherwise humourless mouth. She was a canny woman no doubt. Imbued also with the arrogance of power, he thought. The same everywhere.

"Can I ask you what work you do with the residents here?" Sophia asked.

"We provide both medical and pastoral care for the girls. So it would be highly irregular for an outside doctor to examine one of them."

"I was concerned about some potential complications in her pregnancy."

"Well, that would make you quite the doctor given the limited time that you must have had to examine her previously."

"The first trimester is often the riskiest period for a pregnant woman. Even more so for a girl as young as Collette."

"I am a nurse," said Mother Romana, "and I am quite familiar with pregnancies."

"Are you also a mid-wife?" Sophia asked.

"No. There is a canon law prohibition on nuns being mid-wives. But as I said, we have access to other medical professionals."

"How many residents are there here?" Eamon asked.

"Currently 29."

"That sounds like an expensive operation. How does your order afford it?"

"The County Council pays us a capitation fee for each girl we care for. Our sisters' salaries are also paid for by the authorities. And, of course, some of the girls' families make generous donations for the care of their daughters."

"You said you offered pastoral care to your residents. What is that composed of?" Sophia asked.

"As well as religious instruction we offer them the opportunity to work."

"What sort of work?" Eamon asked.

"Just the sort of thing that many of them would be doing if they were out in the world. Cleaning, cooking, the laundry for the Sisters and the other residents here. Every resident here is required to work for no less than one year."

"Presumably that means the girls are able to save some money to get themselves started once they leave?" Sophia asked.

"No. The girls are unpaid. They are here to atone for their sins, not to plan more of the same gallivanting that got them into trouble in the first place."

There it was, Sophia thought. The judgement. It always amazed her that so many people who claimed to follow the teachings of Jesus often ignored his specific words, *"Neither do I condemn you."*

"So how do the girls take care of their babies when they leave?"

"These girls will offer their children up for adoption to good Catholic homes, somewhere where the taint of their mothers' sins will not be known."

"In Ireland?" asked Sophia.

"And elsewhere, including America. There are good Catholic families everywhere who can offer these children better lives than their mothers ever could. The families that adopt the babies also will make generous donations to help maintain the upkeep of this establishment."

This is like talking to a wimpled brick wall, Sophia thought, and she wondered if Mick might be right about how nuns could spot a Protestant at 200 yards.

"Is it adoption that is planned for Collette's baby?" Sophia asked.

Mother Romana hesitated for a moment. "There is nothing planned for Collette's baby," she said.

"What do you mean?" Sophia asked.

"I am sorry to have to tell you, but Collette Hoey is dead."

135

Sophia felt as if the air had gone out of the room. "How?" she managed.

"She had a haemorrhage. I'm afraid there was nothing to be done."

"When?"

"About ten days ago."

"Had she given any signs beforehand?" Sophia asked.

"She had been complaining of some back and abdominal pain. But naturally we thought she was just trying to malinger."

"So, she was working as your skivvy in spite of complaining of symptoms that, if you were a midwife, you would know are associated with ectopic pregnancy?" Sophia asked.

"As I said, we are concerned here with the pastoral care of our residents as well as their medical needs. I still think it is important that she atoned for her sins."

"She was a child," said Sophia.

"She was a wilful, spiteful child," said Romana with a sudden vehemence. It was as if the mask had finally slipped. "Without hard work and discipline," Romana went on, "she would have become little better than a streetwalker. Perhaps God called her to him now before things got worse and she was lost forever to sin."

"Jesus," said Eamon.

"I'd thank you not to take the Lord's name in vain here, Inspector," Romana said.

"I was praying," said Eamon.

"I sense some disapproval, Inspector," Mother Romana stated.

"Why should you think that?" asked Eamon.

"Ach don't play the innocent with me, Inspector. The girls are here because they have nowhere else to go. When their families and their fancy men want nothing to do with them we take care of them. We provide a service to the state by offering these girls a chance to reform."

"Rendering onto God the things that are Caesar's," said Eamon.

"Many of your colleagues in the Guards would disagree with you, even if you have not learned some of these basic facts of life yet. That is why they will often bring wayward girls to our Sisters in the Magdalene Laundries when they misbehave."

"None of my men will ever do that if I have anything to do with it. It's not for them to usurp the courts."

"You might see it that way, Inspector. But our Sisters provide these girls with another chance that the prison system could never offer them. As we do, they give bold girls a chance to see the error of their ways, to contemplate a better life for themselves."

"How did Collette come to be here?" Sophia asked. "Was it the Guards that brought her?"

"Her father brought her. Poor man. I think he was at his wits end as to what to do with her. Her mother was dead and she was running wild."

"Is that what he told you?" asked Eamon.

"It is."

"And you took him at his word?"

"Of course. Cathal Hoey is a respected member of the community. He was a senior member of the 4th Northern Division of the IRA. Unlike some, he risked his life for Irish freedom."

"And he was one of those who made generous donation to your house for the upkeep of his daughter?"

Romana looked at Eamon for a long moment. "I imagine your work makes you quite cynical, Inspector?"

"I was a battalion commander in Mayo, Mother Superior. I must tell you, some of my comrades I still would not trust further than I could throw them."

"Well, Mr Hoey impressed me as a man of integrity."

"What did Collette say?" asked Sophia.

"I think she rather vindicated Mr Hoey's account. She told some very nasty stories. I could see how the poor man could not cope."

"What stories?" Sophia asked.

"She was a very angry girl when she came here. Annoyed her shenanigans had been curtailed. So we did not pay much heed to them."

"What stories?" Eamon repeated.

"She said her father had interfered with her, that it was him who made her pregnant, and he had put her here just to hush it all up."

"You did not think that could have been true?" asked Sophia.

"We hear many such stories. We have learned to pay them no mind. Mr Hoey is a good Catholic. He was clearly concerned about his daughter. And the girl was clearly just being vindictive because her father had put her here for her own good."

"What good was that? She died here," said Sophia.

"She received the sacraments before she passed. Had she not been here she may not have achieved a state of grace."

"Where is she buried?" Eamon asked.

"In the grounds."

"Can we see the grave?"

"What need is there of that?" Romana asked.

"To pay our respects," said Eamon. "From what you have said it sounds like her soul could do with a few prayers for its repose. It would also provide me a conclusion to my report."

Romana hesitated. Then, "I will permit that."

"Gracious of you," said Eamon. In truth he did not think it was overly gracious of her, but he felt he should still try to stay on her best side, just in case they needed something more from her, the nasty bitch.

"Sophia, I think we have taken up enough of Mother Romana's time."

Sophia looked at him. Eamon could see a simmering fury in her eyes. He wished he could feel some of that too instead of just the empty bleakness that was consuming him now.

Romana arose and opened the door of her office. "Sister Bernadette," she called.

The young nun who had brought them to Romana's office appeared at the door.

"Sister Bernadette, will you please show our guests to the graveyard. They would like to see Collette Hoey's grave," Romana said.

With an effort Sophia pushed herself up from her chair. "Did you inform Collette's father of her death?" she asked.

"Of course," Romana replied.

"So he came for the funeral?"

"No, sadly he was unable to attend. I suspect Collette had brought so much grief to him already that he could bear no more."

XIX

Sister Bernadette ushered Sophia and Eamon down bare, grey corridors towards a stairwell. Halfway down a girl in a cheap smock, who looked to be in her middle teens, was kneeling, scrubbing the floor. She did not look up when she heard their approach but stood and moved herself and her bucket to the turn in the stairs and waited there with her hand crossed before her and her head bowed, a model of dutiful subservience, until the three had passed.

At the base of the stairs a door opened onto a quadrangle. Sister Bernadette led them across the grass towards a path leading to a small chapel. She halted a few yards from the door of the church and pointed towards a space amongst a cluster of graves. "She's there," Sister Bernadette said.

Collette's grave was unmarked. The soil over it was bare of both flowers and grass.

"Thanks, Sister," said Eamon. "I think we can find our own way from here."

Sister Bernadette paused, as if unsure that it would be acceptable to Mother Romana if she were to leave these two unsupervised. Noticing her hesitation, Eamon asked sharply, "Is there something troubling you, Sister?" and fixed her with a hard stare.

"N... no... no," stammered Sister Bernadette. "It's just Mother Romana told me to show you out after."

"I think we can find our own way, thanks."

The young nun still didn't move. "Is there something else?" Sophia asked, considerably more gently than Eamon had managed.

The young nun seemed to be trying to gather up her courage. After a long moment she finally blurted it out. "I was with her when she died," she said.

"With Collette?" asked Sophia.

"Yes," said Sister Bernadette. "I had never seen anyone die before."

"Are you a nurse?" asked Eamon.

"No," said Bernadette. "I was supervising the girls in the kitchen."

"How did it happen?" asked Sophia.

"She was in the scullery washing the pots when she collapsed. She was crying with the pain. We took her to her bed but she was bleeding already. I sent one of the other girls to tell Mother Romana to call the doctor, but Mother Romana wanted to see for herself first. Collette was already grey in the face by the time Mother Romana came to see her."

"Jesus," said Sophia.

"There was so much blood," said Bernadette.

"But no doctor?" asked Sophia.

"The priest arrived before him. He gave her the last rites."

"Skewed priorities," said Sophia with undisguised disgust.

"I'm not sure it would have made much difference," said Bernadette. "I thought she was gone by the time the priest arrived. But he said her spirit still lingered."

"So she didn't quite die in a state of grace, like Mother Romana said?" asked Eamon.

"I can only hope," said Bernadette. "But she was very scared."

"Did you know her well?" asked Eamon.

"Hardly at all," said Bernadette. "While she was dying was really the only time I spoke to her." Bernadette began to cry.

"What did you say to her?" Eamon asked.

"I told her that I had sent for help. I told her everything was going to be okay." Full tears ran down her face now and her body began to shake with sobbing.

Eamon glanced over at Sophia. She was staring at Bernadette with what looked like a mix of horror and compassion. He reached his hand into his jacket pocket and retrieved a white handkerchief. "Here," he said, "it's clean," and handed it to Sister Bernadette. She took it from him, wiped her eyes and blew her nose noisily.

Now it was Eamon's turn to hesitate. But after a moment he moved a little closer towards Bernadette and placed his hand gently on her shoulder. "Why don't you go into the chapel for a few minutes then. You can say a prayer for Collette. We'll wait until you are ready."

Bernadette looked up at Eamon and nodded. In that moment she seemed to him even more of a child than the girl they had just seen scrubbing the stairs.

Sophia and Eamon watched as Bernadette shuffled off wordlessly towards the heavy wooden door of the church and was swallowed up by the darkness within. Then they turned back towards the grave. Eamon made the Sign of the Cross.

"What use are prayers now?" she asked.

"Perhaps nothing," he said. "But you have to do something."

They stood in silence for a few moments more staring at the earth of the grave. "I don't mean to be rude, but is that the best your big detective brain can come up with?" Sophia asked.

Eamon coughed out a mirthless laugh "I must admit to being a bit overwhelmed," he said. Along the side of the graveyard was the looming presence of home's dormitory and refectory. Steam emanated from the windows along with the sounds of the kitchen. But there were few girls' voices and no laughter. Eamon wondered if Mother Romana discouraged talking lest friendships and tenderness made the place more bearable.

"You had never heard tell of places like this before?" Sophia asked.

"I had heard some rumours, I suppose. But they always sounded so benign. Nothing directly in relation to them has ever crossed my desk before."

"Nothing on my side either. I don't know if it's because I've been naive or because it's been kept from the Protestant doctor in case I do not understand your Catholic traditions and noble culture."

Eamon grunted and reached into his pocket for his cigarettes. "Can I have one too?" asked Sophia. Eamon proffered her the pack and the two of them lit up.

"Every man has his dark side. I imagine that applies to every society too."

"Except," said Sophia, "this is a society that has already been traumatised by war and divided by partition. Perhaps that means the dark side of our country will be yet more monstrous as a result. We've both seen how war can turn men into brutes. Perhaps it can do the same to countries?"

"That's a grim prospect," said Eamon. He took a drag on his cigarette. "Ireland become a two-headed hydra," he said, "consuming its young and growing yet more grotesque with every attempt to hack the head off the beast."

"When did you start reading the Greek myths, Eamon?"

"Mick got me properly started on them, years ago. They're miserable."

"Aye. Maybe apt for Ireland then. Doesn't the hydra sprout a couple of new heads for every one that is severed?"

"Aye," said Eamon.

"We're fucked then."

"It certainly looks that way."

Eamon was quiet for a while, his head bowed in contemplation of the grave. After a few minutes Sister Bernadette emerged from the chapel. She had stopped crying but her face was still pale and her eyes red. She had Eamon's handkerchief in her hand and extended it towards him. "Thank you for this," she said.

"That's okay," said Eamon. "Keep it. I have another."

"Thank you," she said again. "Are you ready now? Can I show you out?"

Eamon dropped his cigarette butt on the earth and ground it out with the toe of his boot. Sophia did likewise. "You can," he said to Bernadette. "And thank you. You've been very kind."

"Sure I've done nothing," said Bernadette.

"You were with Collette at the end," said Sophia. "That was a kindness."

For a moment it seemed to Sophia as if Bernadette was going to well up again, but she got herself under control and said simply, "This way if you please."

Eamon and Sophia followed Bernadette back the way that they had come, but rather than ascend the same stairwell, she led them along a different dark corridor to the main entrance of the Home, where she opened the door for them and bade them goodbye.

They held up their hands in farewell to Sister Bernadette as she shut the door of the Home on them. To Eamon's ears the sound resonated like the closing of the gates of a prison.

They turned and walked back towards Sophia's car. Eamon gasped for air. He felt bone weary and his legs were like lead.

"Give us another one of them fags," said Sophia when they got to the car.

"Don't you have any of your own?"

"I finished the last of them waiting for you," she said.

Eamon fished out his cigarettes and the two of them lit up and leaned on the side of the car as they smoked, taking in the grey edifice.

"I don't know about you, Eamon," said Sophia, "but this may be my worst day at work for quite a few years."

"Mine too," he said, "at least since the last time someone tried to kill me."

They smoked on to the ends of the butts, then dropped them to the ground and stamped out the last embers.

"I've had one thought," said Eamon.

"What's that?" asked Sophia.

"There's a Garda station on the Free State side of Jonesborough," he said. "Let's drop in there, see if they have heard anything."

XX

The Garda barracks in Jonesborough was a small, white-washed house at the bottom of a forested hill on the side of the main road to Dublin, just a couple of hundred yards from the border. Sophia pulled up her car beside it.

"Can I come in with you?" she asked.

"Sure why not? We're hardly following strict policing procedures here are we?"

They got out of the car and Eamon adjusted his cap so that it sat straight on his head. Unbidden the words came to Sophia: "the very model of a modern major-general."

"Shall we?" Eamon asked and opened the door to the station for her.

A young guard looked up from behind the station counter as Sophia entered. "Can I help you?" he asked. Then he saw Eamon and, noticing the uniform and the rank, jumped to his feet. "Inspector!" he said.

"Take it easy," said Eamon. "It's just yourself here is it?"

"It is at the moment. The sergeant from Dundalk comes in a couple of times a week, to see how I'm getting on."

"What's your name?"

"Patrick O'Shea."

"Folk call you 'Patrick'?"

"Paddy mostly."

"How long have you been here, Paddy?"

"About six months."

"And how long have you been a guard?"

"Just over a year now."

"Where were you before this?"

"In Dundalk."

"How are you finding village policing?"

"Not too bad. Busy enough. I suppose it helps that I am fairly local."

"You're from Jonesborough?"

"No Faughart."

"Where Edward the Bruce fell."

"The very place."

"So you must be familiar with Cathal Hoey?"

"I am. He's hard to miss in a village this small."

"I heard he was anti-Treaty. Does he give you a hard time for being part of the Free-State police."

"Not really. A village this size, people try to get on."

"So when was the last time you spoke to him?"

"A couple of weeks ago."

"On police business?"

"Yes."

"What was that in relation to?"

Paddy swallowed. "I was enquiring after the whereabouts of his daughter."

"What prompted that enquiry?"

Paddy's eyes flicked towards Sophia.

"Don't worry about her now, Paddy. Dr McGuinness here has worked as a medical examiner. Anything you have to say she'll have heard worse before now." Sophia started slightly at Eamon giving a wrong name for her but said nothing.

"A young fella from Dromintee way."

"Anthony McCreevy?"

"Yes."

"What did Anthony tell you?"

"He told me he was friendly with Collette Hoey."

"And?" Eamon asked.

147

"He told me that there was some folk asking round, saying that Collette had gone missing."

"And so?"

"So, I asked Cathal Hoey about it?"

"And how did that work out for you?"

"No bother really. He told me Collette was fine and that she had gone away to study with the nuns."

"So, you took no further action."

"No."

"Did he tell you where she had gone to study?"

"Em… I'm afraid I didn't ask."

"Did you ask him why she had gone away?"

"Hoey told me Collette had been gallivanting with some young fella so he'd sent her off for her own good."

"Was that all Anthony said to you? That he had heard that Collette had gone missing?"

Paddy hesitated. "Yes," he said.

"You didn't happen to mention to Hoey what prompted your enquiry?"

"I did not."

"Did he ask?"

"He did. But I refused to tell him."

"I hear tell that Hoey can get a bit angry when he doesn't get his own way. How did he react when you refused to tell him who was making the allegations?"

"He got a bit bothered all right, but I explained my duty to him."

"Good man," said Eamon. "Is it okay if I smoke?"

"It is," said Paddy.

Eamon produced a packet of cigarettes from his pocket. "Do you want one yourself," he offered.

"Thanks, Inspector."

Eamon offered a cigarette to Sophia who also took one, and then lit all three. There was a brief moment of communion as they exhaled the blue smoke into the reception room of the small station.

Eamon broke the silence. "You've heard about what happened to Anthony McCreevy?" he asked Paddy.

Paddy swallowed again. "I did."

"Did you revisit Hoey in the light of that?"

"Well, South Armagh is outside of my jurisdiction."

"I am aware of that," said Eamon, "but it happened less than a mile away. Didn't it pique your interest?"

"Well, I didn't see what I could be doing about it."

"Have you heard any stories?"

"What sort of stories?"

"About Anthony. About why someone should do to death such a young fella?"

"There was some story that he had stuff going on with the police in the North."

"What sort of stuff?"

"I mean it's only a rumour, mind, but I heard that he betrayed an arms' dump somewhere."

"And that's why he got himself shot?"

"I mean it's only what I heard."

"But you definitely didn't mention Anthony's name to Hoey."

"I'm not that green, Inspector."

"Good to hear, Paddy."

"Can I ask what this is in relation to, Inspector?"

"I'm making some enquiries."

"What sort of enquiries?"

"The discreet sort."

"Can I ask your name?"

"You can ask, Paddy." Eamon turned to Sophia. "Time for us to be moving on, I think. Unless you want to ask anything of course, Doctor?"

"No, I have no questions, Inspector," Sophia said. "Thank you Paddy. You have been very helpful."

"Well then," said Eamon. "If you can just get the car started, I need a brief private word with Paddy here."

Sophia opened the station door and stepped outside.

Eamon turned back to Paddy.

"This is most irregular," said Paddy.

"Ach, Paddy. If this is the strangest thing you ever see, you'll have led a very dull life. But let me tell you one more thing." Eamon paused as he stubbed out his cigarette in a station ashtray. "If you so much as mention that either me or my friend were here to anyone, either in the Guards or in the community, I know your name and where you live. And if any harm should come to my friend, the doctor there, you are the first person I will come looking for, and I've killed younger men than you for less. So, keep your gob shut about this if you know what is good for you."

Paddy swallowed hard and Eamon could see a sheen of sweat breaking across his brow.

"So, do we understand each other?" Eamon asked.

Paddy nodded.

"Say it," said Eamon.

"I understand, Inspector."

"Good. I hope if we ever meet again it will be under happier circumstances," Eamon said, and then followed Sophia out to the car.

XXI

They drove south only until they were out of sight of the station and then Sophia pulled into the side of the road.

"So, what do you think?" she asked.

"I think I need a drink. Don't you?"

Sophia checked her watch. It was just past four-thirty. "If we drive up to Newry, we can probably catch Mick coming out of work."

"That sounds good. Just let me lose the uniform."

"Grand. Can I just check though. You really didn't bring a revolver with you, did you?"

"I didn't. Much as I might like to, it would be rather unprofessional threatening a nun with a gun, no matter how much she might deserve it."

"Well," said Sophia, "I had to check. I know how you like to have plans for every contingency."

"It is a habit born of combat, I must admit," said Eamon. "But I really couldn't see any scenario evolving today which would have been improved with me shooting somebody."

"Not even shooting Mother Romana?"

"Not even that."

Eamon got out of the car and lifted his satchel from the back seat. "I know you're a doctor so you've seen all sorts, but you probably don't want to look at this," he said.

Eamon threw his cap and uniform jacket onto the back seat and then turned his back to the car. A little curious now, Sophia watched as he removed his uniform shirt and then bent to retrieve a civilian one from his bag. He was lean and well-muscled but there was the jagged mass of scar tissue on his lower back that marked the site of a bullet exit wound.

"Where did you get that?" she asked.

Eamon started. "You're looking so?"

"As a doctor it is always good to stay brushed up on the old anatomical knowledge."

"It's good to hear you are such a diligent student then."

Eamon turned as he finished fastening the buttons of a white shirt.

"So where did you get that wound?"

"France," he said, adjusting his cuffs now.

"Lucky to survive it."

"It would have been luckier never to have been hit," he said, "but there's definitely many have got it worse. Like the first fella who tried to help me."

"What happened to him?"

"Posthumous mention in dispatches."

Eamon tucked the shirt into his trousers. Then he bent and picked up his satchel. He folded his uniform shirt inside of that and then he carried it to the backseat of the car where he set it down on top of his uniform jacket. He closed the back door of the car and climbed back into the front passenger seat.

"No matter how ill I tend to think of the English, and I do think ill of them as a generalised collective, I can never forget how one of their number lost his life trying to save mine. So there is a spark of decency there, if ever it could be fanned into a flame."

"I don't think I will be holding my breath."

"That is, I think, sound medical advice for all of us."

"Was it when you were wounded that you met your wife?" Sophia asked. "When you were recuperating in hospital?"

"When I was recuperating, yes. But not in hospital. Afterwards, in a bar in Paris when I had some leave. Ironically enough, I was actually nursed when I was in hospital by a bunch of nuns."

"What were they like?"

"Lovely women. Very professional, hugely committed. Some of them very funny. You must know what it's like: a lot of folk who deal with life and death every day have to develop a very dry sense of humour to cope. I couldn't think more highly of them to be honest."

"A bit different to Mother Romana so."

"Chalk and cheese with Mother Romana."

"More like Sister Bernadette so?"

"You know, maybe even Mother Romana was once like Sister Bernadette. In life, particularly in organisations, what you become depends an awful lot on how you were led."

"You don't think a *créatúr* like Sister Bernadette is going to end up another Romana?"

"Maybe. Maybe not. Human beings always have some choice in what they become, even if their society does try to limit or determine that choice."

"You've become quite the philosopher since last I saw you, Eamon."

"Always been a reader," he said. "And, in common with Mother Romana, since I was a cub I've known that you should do onto others as you would like them to do onto you. But, whatever way she has been guided in the past it is her choice now to be so thoroughly ignoring it."

"You weren't following the Golden Rule when you tried to kill that fella who took a shot at you."

"I wasn't. But a moment of anger is not the same as a lifetime spent helping build a system of such coldness and cruelty."

"It's not," said Sophia as she put her car into a three-point turn and started north.

"Why didn't you give the young guard your name, and why did you give a false name for me."

"Because I didn't trust him. He said he did not give Anthony's name to Hoey, and yet him ending up dead shortly after Paddy spoke to him is the sort of coincidence I just don't like."

"Red-headed doctors asking questions about Hoey are not going to be too common a commodity."

"I know. But sometimes it's the little things that make the big difference."

"Like a false name?"

"That and a death threat often do the trick?"

Sophia felt her chin drop. "You… you threatened to kill him?" she stammered.

"Only if anything happened to you. Some people need a little extra incentive to keep their mouths shut."

"Jesus, Eamon. What if he reports you to his superiors?"

"I told him that could get him killed too."

"You try to cover all of your bases, don't you?"

"It's not that I like doing it, Sophia. But necessity is the mother of the death threat."

"Why do you think it is so necessary?"

"You told me Hoey threatened to kill you if you came poking around again. From the sound of him he is not the sort to make idle threats. So to my mind it is way better he does not hear you have been poking about."

Sophia was silent for a moment, taking this all in. "So… what do you think?"

"I think you're right. But evidentially it is going to be a complete bastard, even without the jurisdictional issues. Collette seems to have told that bitch over in 'blayney that her Da was her rapist, but she told you something different. God alone knows what she told Anthony, but I think it was enough to get Anthony killed. Anyway, Collette is no longer around to tell anyone anything. So all we have is hearsay and that is not going to get us very far."

"So, two dead children and no one is going to pay the price?"

"That's why I need a drink," said Eamon.

"I think I may be needing a large one too then," said Sophia.

Part Five: Mick

XXII

Sophia and Eamon were waiting for me when I left work. They were leaning on the side of her car and smoking. They waved when they saw me coming out the gate, but there was little cheer in their greetings.

They remained unusually quiet as we drove to a hotel that I knew. There would, I thought, be few people about at that time of day, and it had, as per Sophia's request, wine.

I sat down at a corner table with Sophia while Eamon went to the bar to get drinks.

"So what's the craic?" I asked.

"Wait until Eamon has us the drinks and we'll tell you everything," she said.

I knew things were not good when I saw Eamon knock back a whiskey as he waited on our two pints of porter to settle.

"So," I repeated as Eamon sat down, "what's the craic? Did you get to speak to Collette?"

"No," said Sophia.

"That's a bit frustrating," I said, "after travelling all that way."

"Collette is dead," said Sophia as she lit another cigarette.

"What?"

"She bled to death about ten days ago. From what we heard it sounded like an ectopic pregnancy," Sophia said.

"A what sort of pregnancy?" I asked.

"An ectopic one. It's when the embryo begins to develop in the fallopian tube rather than the uterus. When the inevitable rupture occurs it can be fatal for the mother."

"Jesus," I said.

"My thoughts exactly," said Eamon. He was smoking now too.

"She was in the Mother and Baby home then?" I asked.

"Yes," said Sophia.

"Don't they have facilities there to take care of pregnant girls?"

"The Mother Superior claimed to be a nurse, but she seemed more concerned with punishing Collette for having sex than for seeing to her physical well-being," said Sophia.

"Punishing how?" I asked.

"All the residents are required to work in the home. It sounded to me as if they are used as domestic servants. The Mother Superior said it is part of the pastoral care that they provide for the girls," said Sophia. "When Collette complained of abdominal pain the nuns thought she was malingering."

"Jesus," I said, "but outside of an army or the police you don't expect to have to risk your life to earn a living."

"I don't think the girls resident in the home were earning much of a living. It sounded rather that they are unpaid. The nuns seem to think that board and lodgings and what passes for medical care is sufficient for them," said Eamon.

"Why do they put up with that?" I asked.

"They have nowhere else to go," said Sophia. "Their families have turfed them out for supposedly bringing 'shame' on them, though for my money they're the ones acting shamefully. So the girls are acutely vulnerable, and that vulnerability has been disgracefully abused without compunction by them who have been given the power to act as judge, jury and in Collette's case, executioner over them."

"Like prisoners," said Eamon.

"I can think of another analogy," I said.

"What's that?" asked Eamon.

"Well, confined against their will, to work for no pay, with no concern for their physical well-being: didn't Lincoln fight a war to end that sort of thing?"

"Quite the new Ireland," said Sophia, and drank down some of her wine. "Was this the smallest glass they had, Eamon?"

"I can get you another when you need," he replied.

"What happens to the babies that survive?" I asked.

"They are put up for adoption for Catholic families, who seem to pay for the privilege."

"But isn't there a law against these sorts of things?" I asked.

"You mean slavery?" asked Eamon. "You were the law student. Can you not tell us?"

"I have not had access to many legal books while locked up inside."

"It doesn't matter what the law says," said Sophia.

"Of course it does," I said. "It is sort of foundational to the concept of 'rule of law'."

"Ah Mick," she said, "I think you may be on the verge of learning something that women have known for centuries."

"What's that?" I asked.

"That if you think the 'rule of law' is for you, then you are setting yourself up for a lifetime of terrible disappointment."

"But isn't that what we were fighting for, Eamon?"

"Some of us certainly were," said Eamon. "The whole idea took a bit of a hammering during the Civil War though, with both sides behaving like the Black and Tans sometimes."

"Too long a suffering can make a stone of the heart," said Sophia. "It's forlorn to hope for anything better now."

"You told me I was the despairing one," I said.

"Well then," she said, "allow me a moment of that luxury," and she took another gulp of wine.

"Look, I'm not a lawyer, just a humble doctor," she said, "but with partition the British have intentionally created a state for the Protestant Supremacists to reign over in the North. So, by default, they have created a confessional Catholic state in the South. Without substantial Protestant representation in the Dáil, there will be little brake on the excesses of the Catholic Church there, just as being left to their own devices, the Protestant majority in the North show every intention of lording it over the Catholic minority here for as long as they can get away with it." Sophia took a sip of her wine.

"It is not power that corrupts, per se," she went on. "It is unconstrained power, and that is what the British partition of Ireland has ensured, in both states. And the English will do nothing about it. Irish people shooting each other, poor Catholics being deprived of decent housing or their most basic rights in a part of their Kingdom is less important to their ruling classes—Left or Right—than the racing at Ascot, or, for their working classes, than the football scores on a Saturday."

"All of them?" I asked.

"Enough as to make no difference," said Sophia. "Like the British Empire, the United Kingdom has always been principally an English project. The Irish and the Scots, even the most loyal Protestant ones, are just tolerated for when the English need the cannon fodder. And England is a country that spoon feeds its kids Rudyard Kipling. So, they grow up thinking they are special and no one else on Earth really matters."

"So what does all this mean in relation to the Mother and Baby homes?" I asked.

"It means," said Sophia, "that the worst excesses of the intolerant portion of the Catholic Church are likely to be given free rein now in the Free State. Already they are talking about banning divorce down South. How can any plural society justify that unless it is doing the bidding of a theocratic tendency. And those self-same theocrats know about what is happening to those girls in those homes and are not going to do anything about it so long as the people of Ireland let them get away with it."

"But this is slavery," I said. "Surely we are better than that?"

"It is only slavery if we call it slavery. Mother Romana called it 'pastoral care.' That's just the sort of euphemism that people love to help them swallow an atrocity. You think the Crusaders who butchered innocent Muslims and Jews in Palestine on their way to seize Jerusalem called what they were doing 'murder'? Not at all, they called it 'pilgrimage' and treated it as a moral good. And the Crusaders are on the march again, South and North. The light of the true believer burned as bright in the eyes of Mother Romana as it did in the eyes of Inspector Hanby. And there are many more will be happy to acquiesce in their absolute certainties, so long that is, that they are not the victim of those certainties."

"So where does this leave us," I asked.

"The Mother Superior…" Eamon began.

Sophia interrupted him. "…is a cunt," she said.

"She is," said Eamon. "But she also told us that before she died Collette had alleged that her father had raped her. The Mother Superior said she never paid her much heed as she was, if I recollect her words correctly, 'an angry and wilful girl'."

"Jesus," I said, "if I had been raped and ended up being locked up instead of the rapist, I think I would be pretty angry too."

"Fortunately for you, Mick, that's a situation that no man is ever likely to have to face," said Sophia.

"We also found out," Eamon said, "that Anthony had reported Cathal Hoey to the Guards in Jonesborough."

"Do you think the Guards touted Anthony out to Hoey then?" I asked.

"The Guard in question denied it, but that seems to me the most likely scenario," Eamon said.

"And that Collette confided in Anthony?"

"Again I would guess that is so," said Eamon. "But we don't have enough evidence to prove it even if we could surmount the jurisdictional issues."

"So how do we get more evidence?" I asked.

"That's a good question. In relation to Anthony, the RUC are in no position to put their hands on Hoey to use their methods of gentle persuasion to get him to talk," said Eamon. "In relation to Collette, the nuns have literally buried the crime scene. Anthony is not around to support her story. Her Da will deny it. It will also be problematic that she told Sophia a wholly different story, that of Anthony being the father, when she met her."

"And," said Sophia, "don't forget, Cathal Hoey is an aristocrat of the revolution. A senior IRA officer. Did you see Mother Romana simpering over the thought of him. His pals, his acolytes, for fuck sake just about the whole community will close ranks about him out of fawning adoration, or fear, or both."

"So," I said, "stalemated?"

"It's been a while since I've played chess, Mick," said Eamon, "but it's beginning to seem a lot more like 'zugzwang' to me: any move that we make will just fuck the situation up worse than it already is."

"But isn't the rule that we have to move anyway?" I asked.

"Or we can resign," said Eamon. "Sometimes there is nothing to be done."

"There is something else we are forgetting," said Sophia.

"What is that?" I asked.

"There is still another daughter in that house," she said.

I remembered the timid girl who had fetched her father when we had visited what seemed a very long time ago. "You think Cathal has moved on to his second daughter after causing the death of his first," I asked.

"It hardly seems likely that he will be troubled by conscience in that regard," said Sophia, and drained her glass. "A proper sized one this time," she said handing the glass to Eamon. Eamon wordlessly took it from her.

"Wait," I said. "It's my round."

"It is," said Eamon, and handed me the glass.

I went up to the bar and asked for a large glass of wine and, even though neither myself nor Eamon had finished our pints, two more of those. I watched Eamon and Sophia talking quietly to each other as they sat at the table looking out the window on the hotel garden. There seemed to be a certain ease about them, old acquaintances who just picked up where they left off even after years. I wondered for a moment if, maybe, they had been closer than that in the years after I joined the flying column. When I knew him Eamon was often closed lipped about much of his personal life at the best of times, and I hadn't seen him in years.

I carried the drinks back to the table and sat down. "Thanks, Mick," they said in unison.

"So what do you think we should do now?" I asked them.

"I am not sure there are any legal routes open to us," said Eamon.

I took a slug out of my pint. "There are other routes," I said.

"Not anymore," said Eamon.

"There's another girl still in that house," I said.

"No," said Eamon.

"What are you talking about?" asked Sophia.

"You've not always been so squeamish," I said to Eamon.

"Well, I think now is definitely a good time to start," Eamon said.

"What the fuck are youse two talking about?" asked Sophia.

Eamon looked at her. "You know yourself, Sophia. The IRA has had a tradition that might be called 'extrajudicial'."

166

Sophia's gasp was audible. "Jesus, Mick! No!" she said.

"Two dead children and no justice. Are we to wait for a third and still no justice?" I asked.

"You are not talking about justice here, Mick," said Sophia, "but vengeance."

"That might do me for the moment," I said.

"An eye for an eye, like?" asked Sophia.

"Aye," I said.

"Until the whole world goes blind?" asked Sophia.

"For the now, I'm just thinking about the one," I said.

"What after that then? Are you going to cycle over to Castleblayney and start shooting nuns?" Eamon asked. "There is a whole system here. We've already seen how limited violence has been in bringing justice to this land, and that is when we had most of the nation behind us. What chance do you think you might have with just a revolver and a bicycle?"

Eamon was looking at me with some intensity now. "I have to carry the deaths of all the men I have been responsible for in my conscience until the day I die," he said, "and I may have to answer for them then. So I am not planning on adding more if I can possibly avoid it."

"And what about the screams of raped children?" I asked. "What about the weeping of enslaved girls? How do those sit on your conscience now?"

"Dreadfully. But these are things you are not going to fix with a bullet. Doing Hoey, that is at least a three man job if you want to be sure that you do it right and hope for any chance of getting away with it. Even if I was to go along with that, and I will not, we are still one short unless you were thinking about enlisting Sophia as wheelman?

167

"And as for the Mother and Child homes," Eamon went on, "waste even the nastiest of nuns and the hue and cry that would meet that would have you lynched before any cop could put their hands on you."

"I wasn't talking about shooting nuns."

"No. But it's the logical extension of where you are at right now. And that brings you to a place of utter madness."

I took another pull on my pint. "Yes, you are probably right," I said. "That's what my head says too. But my gut is saying something different. Like how a bullet could end at least some of this."

Sophia reached out her hand and placed it on mine. "Give it time," she said. "You've done what you can do, Mick. You must move on otherwise this all could consume you too."

"Indeed," I agreed. "But I just hope that my path does not cross with that of Hoey on some moonless night."

"It's good that you are thinking about fighting for others again, Mick. But there's ways that are more suited to the times than violence," said Eamon.

"There are solicitors in Newry, Mick. Maybe you can get a clerkship with one of them," said Sophia.

"What sort of solicitor is ever going to employ an ex-jailbird like me?" I asked.

"I may be mistaken, Mick, but I don't think you actually have a criminal record. You were interned weren't you?" asked Sophia.

"Yes."

"So you have never actually faced a judge on a charge of anything?"

"No."

"So maybe all hope is not yet lost for a legal career. I can speak to my own lawyer, and there's another is a patient of mine. We can see what the options are," said Sophia. "There's more ways to fight than with a gun."

"And remember this, Mick. Fuckers like Hoey always make a mistake eventually. I can promise you that. We'll get him when that happens," said Eamon.

I said nothing, but this still seemed so wrong to me. It was not just the thought of Collette bleeding to death with no one who loved her near. It was the guilt I felt for Anthony, and the thought if I had talked to him in a different way, or not at all, he might still be alive today.

Eamon looked at his watch. "I had better be moving if I want to catch the train," and he skulled back the rest of his pint.

"We'll be grand," said Sophia, "It'll only take me five minutes to run you over to the station."

"I'll say goodbye to you now then," I said standing up and offering my hand to Eamon, "I need to pick up my bike and my Ma will be worrying if I am out too much longer."

"Look, Mick," he said as he took my hand, "I know this is miserable. But as you must know by now sometimes that's the best that can be achieved. But at least we are not strangers anymore. Come to Dublin again before the end of the summer. We can have a game of chess over a pint while Sophia can go and look at dresses or shoes."

Sophia snorted at the perceived slight.

"Go to see a play or something too," said Eamon, as if in recompense for reducing Sophia's intellectual interests to the fashions of the day.

"That would be great," I said.

"It would," said Sophia.

Eamon slapped me on the shoulder. "Stay strong, Mick," he said, "and keep the faith."

"What faith is that?" I asked.

"That, so long as we are not dead, we can still change the world," he said.

I walked with them to the car park. "Can I drop you somewhere?" asked Sophia.

"No thanks," I said. "I think I could do with a bit of a walk."

"So long then, Mick," said Eamon. "I'll be seeing you again soon."

"Go well," I said, and waved at them in the car as Sophia started the engine. She managed a wave back before she turned towards the gate. I watched as they drove out onto the road and towards the train station. Then I started the walk back towards the abattoir where my bicycle was locked up.

Saturday 6 June 1925

XXIII

After breakfast I took out the bicycle for a spin to clear my head. I cycled up past the cairn at Clontigora, which, I knew, were places that my stone age ancestors had buried their people. But I still enjoyed the stories of the 'fairy forts' associated with such places. Many of the 'hollow hills' like this had been plundered for their stone to ease the construction of the Newry Canal.

I wonder if the Italians had cannibalised the Colosseum to build Venice because the devastation that the canal engineers had wreaked on these ancient sites was as bad as that. Still, this particular place had survived the vandalism a bit better than most. Nevertheless, I often hoped that those who had quarried places like these were plagued with the bad luck and lumbago that the legends warned about.

I took a back road to avoid the border posts before turning onto the main Dublin Road. I passed Jonesborough and cycled up into Ravensdale where I paused for a while under a tree and amid a patch of bluebells. I took a long drink from my water bottle as I took in the view of the valley rippling under the shadows of the shifting clouds.

But bucolic as the scene was, I had too much on my mind to find it relaxing. Mounting up again, I decided if not to confront, then at least to reconnoitre the beast.

I cycled back up to Jonesborough and through the village towards the Hoey farm. I paused a few hundred yards out and leaned my bicycle against the post of a gate to a field where some cattle were grazing. I pulled out my field glasses. There was no sign of him, or indeed of any activity, in the yard and garden around his house.

Eamon had said it was a three-man job, including a car, if you wanted a proper chance to finish him and get away with it. I wondered. One man with a rifle could probably do it from a bit of a distance and get away easy enough. But I didn't have a rifle.

Reggie Dunn and Joe O'Sullivan had killed Field Marshall Sir Henry Wilson, an MP and military adviser to the Northern Ireland government, in broad daylight in London but could not escape on foot from the mob that gathered in the immediate aftermath of the assassination. Perhaps, if all that was available was revolvers, a night attack would offer more chance of escape. But how to predict where he would be vulnerable to an attack and when? Of course, you could just knock the door of his house, but that would risk witnesses, as would any prolonged reconnaissance. But for one man alone the only chance would be to take up a concealed position and stake him out, and to wait... and wait... and wait until an opportunity presented itself. Even then any careful assassin would have to be ready to abort the whole thing if circumstances changed unfavourably.

I stowed away the glasses and remounted my bike. Out of curiosity, as I had not been there since I got out of jail, I cycled up to Adavoyle, where, back in 1921, the 4th Northern Division had ambushed a train carrying British cavalry and their mounts on their way back to Dublin having escorted the King to the opening of the Protestant parliament in Belfast.

There was little sign of it now, but back then there had been bloody carnage all around the place that I now stood. The IRA had managed to derail the train as it passed over the viaduct and, in the attack, four soldiers had been killed, and most of their horses. There would have been more but, so I was told in jail, the men tasked with lighting a fire to signal to the attackers on the line that the train was approaching, had difficulty with their kindling. So, the attack had gone off mistimed.

I tried to imagine the chaos of wounded men and screaming horses in the aftermath of the assault. I wondered also if things had gone as planned, if they had managed to kill more of the troops, would it have changed the political realities on this island in any meaningful way? Even if such a thing could not have prevented partition would it have forced the border a little further northward, keeping this portion of south Ulster outside of the Orange state?

It was one of those imponderables, I supposed. But somehow I doubted now that it would have had much effect. The British had their own agenda and the welfare of Irish people, indeed anybody outside of their ruling classes, was not high upon it. And Lloyd George and his government had their own political pressures, particularly from the right-wing of the Tory party who had taken it upon themselves to do the bidding of the Protestant Supremacists who now ruled the North.

So, the Free State as it was constituted was probably the high-water mark of what war could have achieved, and those of us in the North who had hoped for an all-Ireland state, where Orange and Green would be united in peace and equality, were left high and dry as the tide of war had ebbed away.

But maybe the war itself had rendered the notion of a united Ireland a more distant hope? How, after all, can you unite a people at the point of a gun? Would there ever be enough time to heal the wounds that we had inflicted upon each other?

Sophia had once said, years ago, in Mayo, that after the grief for the casualties of war fades the bitterness remains, particularly in a civil war. She was right. And now we in the North were left to reap that bitterness, while the Free Staters and the English would tell themselves in the coming years that what went on up here had nothing to do with them.

I decided to head for home. I cycled back towards the Dublin Road. Just past Cloughoge I rounded a corner and almost collided with a RUC roadblock, unusually on a side road, rather than the main one.

"Hold up there," said the peeler on point.

I stopped. It was Constable Jeffrey, one of the cops who had given me the kicking during my sojourn in the Newry police barracks.

"Well, well, well," he said, "fancy meeting you here."

"I live round here," I said.

"Just out for a spin then?"

"Yes."

"Off the bike, McAlinden," he said.

I dismounted and set the bicycle on the ground.

"Hands over your head."

I did as I was told.

Constable Jeffrey gave me a quick body search, and finding nothing interesting asked, "What's in the bag?"

I opened my satchel for his inspection. He had a look: *Don Quixote*, a water bottle and the field glasses. He took those out.

"British Army issue. Where did you get these?"

"A Black and Tan gave them to me. He had no more use for them."

"Are you taking the pish?"

"Not at all. I think he wanted to show no hard feelings, like."

"Easy for them boys to say. They don't have to live here with youse."

"But you don't have to live with us either, Constable. I'm sure a man with your experience would have no difficulty getting employment with the police over the water if you wanted."

"I don't," said Constable Jeffrey, "I've seen England and much prefer to live here among the decent people of Ulster than the mongrel races infesting their cities."

Jeffery had a further rummage around in my bag in case he had missed something. "So, what were you doing with the binoculars?" he asked.

"A bit of bird watching."

"Really?"

"Aye."

"You find crows that interesting?"

"There are some raptors around Ravensdale."

"Really?"

"Aye." I had never seen any myself, but our Joe had told me that one had flown low over him as he cycled that way early one morning.

"What sort?"

"That's what the glasses are for."

Constable Jeffrey grunted and stuffed them back in the bag.

"What's the book about?" he asked.

"It's about two fellas trying to make the world a better place."

"Do they succeed?"

"Of course not."

Constable Jeffrey grunted and pushed the bag back towards me.

"On your way then," he said.

I slung the satchel over my shoulder, remounted my bike and pushed away from the roadblock. There were about half a dozen other cops positioned between their vehicles and the ditches, with carbines at the ready, warily scanning the countryside.

"And remember," Constable Jeffrey shouted after me as I headed for home, "keep your nose clean!"

Monday 15 June 1925

XXIV

This time, they did not wait for me to leave work. A squad of peelers with carbines and drawn revolvers barged into the abattoir in the middle of the morning. I was using a yard brush to sweep up but, as soon as I saw them, I dropped it and extended my hands over my head as far as they would go.

This time Hanby had come personally. "I think we need to have a little chat, Michael, don't you?"

XXV

"Did I not tell you to keep your nose clean?" Hanby started.

We were sitting in his office. I was handcuffed but the lack of arms on the chair I was sitting in this time allowed for a greater degree of comfort than before. Hanby had a manila folder open in front of him and a lit cigarette in his mouth.

"That's what I've been doing," I said.

"Really?"

"Really."

Now I know I've said that the first rule of interrogations in situations like this was to keep your mouth shut. But for some reason, given my previous encounters with Hanby, this did not seem appropriate to me now.

"Want to explain to me something awkward then?" asked Hanby.

"What might that be?" I asked.

"Cathal Hoey," Hanby said.

"From our last conversation," I said, "you seem to know more about him than I do."

"That may well be the case," said Hanby, "apart from one small detail."

"And what small detail is that?" I asked.

"How Hoey ended up dead yesterday morning?"

I swallowed but said nothing.

"So now you start with the silence stratagem?" asked Hanby. "I mean I don't want to tell you IRA boys your jobs, but you should have started with that one when first we met."

Hanby started reading from the folder. "Body found yesterday morning, Armagh side of Jonesborough. Initial medical examination suggest that he was killed sometime in the early hours of that morning. Can you account for your whereabouts?"

"I want a solicitor," I said.

"Haven't we been over this before, Michael? You can want all you want. I have the Emergency Powers Act, and you are not getting a solicitor. You'll be lucky not to get a kicking from the constables, just for old times' sake, if we cannot clear this up before too long."

Hanby took a long drag on the end of his cigarette, blew a cloud of blue smoke into the air and then stubbed out the butt.

"Saturday 6th June," Hanby read from another page, "you were stopped in the vicinity of Jonesborough, with a pair of field glasses in your bag. What were you up to? A bit of reconnaissance and planning?"

"I live in Killean. Everywhere around there is in the vicinity of Jonesborough."

"And the field glasses?"

"Bird watching," I said.

Hanby let out a laugh. "Lord Almighty," he said, "but is that the best you could come up with?"

I said nothing and Hanby lit another fag. As he drank in the smoke he seemed to have decided upon a slightly different tack.

"Look, I know Hoey was a bad bastard. No court is going to look too unfavourably upon a man that brought him to justice in the end."

"If you think it was justice, why are you trying to pin it on me? Should you not be offering me a medal?"

"Do you think you deserve that medal?" Hanby asked.

"That's not what I said. It's just that it seems a bit hypocritical to be pursuing Hoey's killer with such vigour if you thought it right that he should be dead."

"I don't know if I have explained it to you before, but my role is upholding the law, not adjudicating justice. That is for the judges."

My mouth was dry. "Can I have some water please?" I asked.

"What about a cup of tea?"

"Thank you."

Hanby burst out laughing. "The only thing you will be getting off me if you do not start answering questions, is another beating."

"What questions do you want answers for?"

"How did you do it?"

"I didn't."

Hanby picked up the folder again and began to read, "Two gunshot wounds to the back. One between the shoulder blades, one to the back of the head." He looked up at me, "That sounds to me like close quarters work with a hand gun: one to put him down and one to finish him off. Ever kill anybody like that, Michael?"

I said nothing.

"We haven't got the ballistics report yet," Hanby went on, "but I'm prepared to bet a .38 calibre weapon was used, maybe a Webley. You don't happen to have a .38 calibre Webley in your possession, do you Michael?"

"Of course not."

"I've come across a lot of such killings over the past few years," said Hanby.

"Some of them even by the peelers, I imagine."

"Ah, whataboutery! I'm afraid it doesn't work like that in this situation. Just because our lot have done a few does not give you license to do a few more back."

"I never thought it did," I said. "I was just highlighting the hypocrisy again."

"Yes," said Hanby. "There is a certain logic to that. But you are again missing one small, awkward detail."

"And what small detail is that?" I asked.

"We won," he said. "Whatever dreams of a Romish Republic you lot may have had, we have put a stop to them in this portion of Ulster. So I get to decide what we are going to talk about, what sort of killings I'm going to look at, and who I'm going to talk to about them."

"Well, enjoy it while you can," I said. "The Boundary Commission may have something to say about whether this portion of south Ulster is even within Northern Ireland a few months from now."

Hanby let out another laugh. "You know the Boundary Commission is constituted with one member nominated from the Free State, one from Northern Ireland, and one from Britain."

"I do."

"Well, you should know then that two is more than one? Collins and Griffith were supposed to be the smart ones and yet they missed that crucial little gerrymander in the Treaty when it was right there in front of their noses. There is going to be no change in the border. Northern Ireland is Protestant, and you should know by now, what Protestants have we hold."

"A gerrymander hardly seems a sound basis for political stability to me."

"Sure half of Europe has had its borders redrawn this way in the Versailles Settlement. Why should Ireland be any different?"

"And look at the carnage that has befallen central and eastern Europe as a result of that."

"I think those of us who were on the Somme will not be daunted by threats of carnage. So you can whinge all you like if you feel that the fate of the Sudeten Germans has befallen you, and you have ended up on one side of a border when you would prefer the other. But that is hardly going to change the political realities."

"One third of the population of Northern Ireland is not Protestant. You don't think that is going to pose you a problem in the future."

"We are used to siege and warfare since we took this land from your forefathers who were too weak to hold it. So we are used to uppity Fenians. I think we can manage our affairs. Particularly now that we have finally gotten free rein from the English. They are not going to be bothered about what we do to keep order here so long as we do it quietly and it doesn't bother them."

"It doesn't sound very much like a healthy society to me," I said.

"Depends what you mean by a 'healthy society'," said Hanby as he stubbed out the end of his cigarette. "In my book that is a society in which Fenians know their place. If we had wanted it different we would be in your mongrel Free State already. But that nonsense is against God and nature. Do you expect us to treat the horse as the equal of the rider too?"

"Human beings are not horses."

"No. A horse knows its place. And you will be taught to know yours, even if we have to break you to do so. The English will ensure we keep our borders intact. And we've started as we mean to continue: a bit more tinkering with the electoral boundaries of parliamentary seats and council districts will keep power in our hands from here on out. So, it's best if you learn good manners if you want to continue living here."

"You will reap a whirlwind."

Hanby lit another cigarette. "I doubt it. But we digress. We were discussing how you are going to be spending the next twenty years of your life in one of His Majesty's prisons—if you are lucky, that is, and they don't decide to hang you."

"I did not kill Hoey," I said.

"But I think we have established that you have killed loyal British subjects, and frankly that is good enough for me. Christmas is coming early this year. I am able to tie the killing of one perpetrator of Altnaveigh with another."

I looked at him in disbelief. "I had nothing to do with Altnaveigh."

"You were in the IRA," he said.

"In Mayo."

"And yet you were arrested in South Armagh just a few weeks after Altnaveigh."

"I had nothing to do with Altnaveigh," I said.

"The people of Altnaveigh had little to do with anything, but that didn't protect them did it?"

"In June 1922, I had just arrived home to visit my family. I was not involved in any of the activities of the 4th Northern Division against Altnaveigh or any other targets."

"So how did you feel when you heard about it."

"I felt sick. It was not the sort of war I ever wanted to fight."

"And yet so many of your comrades were fine with it. At least thirty men were involved. The roads were cut isolating the area from relief by the police, the area surrounded, the residents hunted down for no crime other than being Protestants. Six dead in the end, multiple wounded, houses burned down. But if they had been half competent gunmen they would more likely have killed thirty."

"Maybe that means they had little stomach for it."

"Oh they had plenty of stomach for it. I saw that with my own eyes."

I blinked for a moment, taking that in. "You were there?" I asked.

"I was there," he said, "visiting my parents."

"How did you survive it?"

"I was left for dead. I had one bullet in me, but I had also been splashed with so much of my parents' blood and flesh that I looked a hopeless case. Final thing my parents did for me, I suppose."

"How old were they?" I asked.

"My father was sixty-five. My mother was sixty."

"I am sorry for your loss," I said.

"Fuck off," said Hanby, his eyes glittering with the fury of just vengeance. "I do not want your sympathy. I want your conviction. Just as I want to see all of your like in jail until you rot."

When I first heard of Altnaveigh it had sounded like a disgrace to me, the sort of savagery we would condemn the Black and Tans for. I had heard some more talk of it in jail from some of the South Armagh Volunteers, some of whom were there, some of whom were elsewhere and got it at second hand.

One of the stories was that Altnaveigh was an Ulster Volunteer Force community and home to many of the B-Specials involved in the atrocities against the local civilian Catholic population that had occurred in the previous days. Another story was that it was a regrettable necessity to discourage such attacks in the future. The Germans had done similar things in Belgium. The British had, of course, done such things over and over again in Ireland. So there was precedent amongst so-called civilised armies for such actions. It was the logic of war when the civilian population was as much a part of the struggle as the armed forces. But once those dogs were unleashed, would it ever be possible to restrain them again?

However, much as I had come to detest Hanby I could not help but feel pain for him, imagining myself in similar circumstances with my own parents, shivering in the cold, waiting for the end at the hands of bigoted neighbours baying for blood.

"Hoey was the on-the-ground commander at Altnaveigh," said Hanby.

"Did you see him there?"

"No. But it has been confirmed by the interrogations of multiple of your comrades. There may be honour amongst thieves, but it appears there is fuck all amongst Fenians."

Hanby was revelling in this moment. I had seen such things before: how some gloried in their moral certainty and relished it when the moment came to pass judgement. For folk like that, the certainty of the rightness of a cause could excuse any means they chose. That was probably what the men who did the killing at Altnaveigh told themselves to get to sleep at night, when they were troubled, as I hoped they would always be, by the weeping of the doomed.

"You know," I tried, "Altnaveigh hardly occurred in a vacuum. It was not the first atrocity in South Armagh. As well you know, it was preceded by the murder of Catholic civilians in Derrymore, and the rape of Catholic women in Dromintee. You try to taint me with guilt by association with the IRA. But those outrages were both perpetrated by your colleagues in the police. Do you feel as angry about those as you do about Altnaveigh?"

"Terrible things happen in wars."

"That's it then? In times of war the laws fall silent?"

"Thus has it always been."

"Well, you can hardly be surprised if some follow your example then, can you?"

"Who was following who's example? The Protestant people of Ulster still remember the slaughter visited upon us by your forebearers in 1641. We have been fighting for our very survival in this province for three hundred years. In that time we have learned what needs to be done to keep the jackals from the door."

"Jesus," I said. "So, if we ignore the entire Elizabethan conquest of Ulster, and how Mountjoy scorched the very earth of these parts, starving to death thousands of women and children in the process, it was the Catholics who started all this bloodshed three hundred years ago. That means your atrocities are always fine because they are always in reaction to some things that Catholics did first. But our atrocities are always uniquely odious?"

"Our cause is true and just. Your cause is Romish tyranny."

"So the ends justify the means?"

"Thus has it always been," said Hanby.

"What if there is no end? What if all that you have is the means? Does that still make you Godly and true? Or someday will you awaken to discover that all your means have done is created a bloody labyrinth that you are as lost in as the rest of us and your face is that of the monster you thought you had already butchered quietly in the dark."

Hanby smiled at that. "I am impressed at how your classical education seems to come to the fore in situations of extremity, Michael. Maybe those Christian Brothers are good for something after all. But Theseus is perhaps not the best allusion for you to choose here. You will recall that he went on to rule Athens for many years, irrespective of how well or badly his conscience troubled him. I learned in France to carry my share of dark memories. If I have to carry a few more to ensure that the Protestant people of Ulster survive and prosper, it is a burden I am willing to take up. It is how I will serve this state and see it thrive."

The prejudice of the highly intelligent can be even more impervious than that of the stupid. Hanby had constructed the defences of his irrationality so elaborately that it was like trying to argue with South Armagh basalt.

I could not think where to turn next in this conversation, so I asked again, "Can I have some water, please?"

Hanby looked at me in silence. Finally he shouted, "Constable Wilson!"

There was the clump of booted footsteps in the next door office and then on the corridor outside, and one of the peelers who had given me a kicking appeared at the door.

"Constable," said Hanby, "bring me a jug of water and two glasses please. At the double."

"Yes sir," said Constable Wilson and he disappeared from the door.

"Let us start from the beginning shall we?" said Hanby, and he consulted his notes again. "At the beginning of May, the 9th to be precise, you were involved in an altercation with Hoey, from the looks of which you came off the worse for wear."

"Hardly a motive for murder."

"Your Doctor Hennessy told us you were assisting her in an attempt to locate a patient who had missed her appointment."

"Yes."

"And that patient was Collette Hoey, Cathal's daughter?"

"Yes."

"Did you ever locate Collette?"

"She was in a Mother and Baby home in Castleblayney."

"How did she get there?"

"Her Da put her there. Said she was gallivanting and she had become pregnant."

"So a happy ending of sorts to that story then."

I wondered if I should tell him that no, it wasn't such a happy ending but instead I said, "Again hardly a motive for murder."

There was a firm knock on the door. "Enter," shouted Hanby, and Constable Wilson entered carrying a tray with a jug of water and two glasses. He set it on Hanby's desk.

"Would you like to give the prisoner something to drink?" Hanby asked Wilson. Wilson smiled, filled a glass and brought it towards me. I just about managed to get my lips to the rim before Wilson heeled the contents over me. I barely got a mouthful down, but it was something. I shook the spilled water out of my face as Hanby and Wilson laughed uproariously.

"Thank you, Constable Wilson. That will be all. Leave the water," said Hanby.

Wilson, still chuckling, closed the door behind him and left us alone again.

"Glad to be the source of some amusement to youse," I said.

"And I'm grateful for it," said Hanby.

"For folk who claim to be British you don't seem much enamoured with the idea of British fair play."

Hanby burst out laughing. "In the name of the Almighty," he said, "but where did you get this notion of British fair play? We have conquered half of the globe. You think we did that with cricket and games of dominoes? The empire is for the benefit of the mother-country. We will leave the scraps for the natives so long as they know their place. Do you know your place, Michael?"

"Plainly not," I said.

"Yes, I saw that about you when first we met and knew you were going to be a problem."

"You told me to keep my nose clean and that is what I have done."

"And yet, here I am still, with two dead bodies unaccounted for." He stubbed out his fag.

We looked at each other through the cigarette smoke, and I had the sense that Hanby was just toying with me, like the proverbial cat with the mouse. I had once seen a cat play with a mouse. My Da told me that the fear this caused in the mouse made its meat taste sweeter to the cat. If I did not want to be consumed by Hanby's system I needed to try and shift the dynamic of this conversation.

"I think Hoey killed Anthony," I said.

"What makes you say that?"

"Anthony reported that Collette was missing to the Guards at Jonesborough. I think that he also had some suspicions as to the parentage of Collette's baby."

"What sort of suspicions?"

"The incestuous sort."

Hanby looked at me for a minute and blinked. "God help us, but you Fenians really are doomed for eternal hellfire, and rightly so." He stood up from behind his desk and lit himself another cigarette, sucking deep and then blowing smoke at me. Even for a smoker, I thought, he is doing a lot of smoking. What sort of pressure is he under? I wondered.

"So you think the Guards let slip what Anthony had been saying and that was enough to get him killed."

"I would also imagine, Inspector, that you would not take it well either if someone was putting it about town that you had been fucking your own mother before she died."

Hanby moved quickly from behind his desk and struck me so hard in my mouth that he knocked me clean out of my chair, which also went clattering onto the floor. I rolled away from it as quickly as I could, sure that he would also be putting the boot in while I was on the floor. But he restrained himself and I saw him shaking his hand to take the sting out of his knuckles as I struggled to my feet.

"You see my point, Inspector. Touch on some raw nerves and even the most disciplined of men lose control."

Hanby picked up my chair and set it back on its legs. "Sit down," he said.

I did as he commanded and he returned to his seat behind the desk.

"Let me presume for a moment that your theory is correct, that Hoey killed Anthony because he was bad mouthing him. That still leaves me with Hoey to account for, and you have just confessed to a motive."

"Really?" I asked.

"Really," he said.

"Enlighten me so."

"Enraged at the heinous murder of young Anthony McCreevy, you decided to even the score."

"Really, Inspector. You disappoint me. Even with the most biased judge in the country, and I'm sure you have such men in your back pocket, that will sound desperately thin. I met the young fella once. Nice kid, gutsy. But that is hardly a reason that I would risk my liberty to avenge him."

"Maybe you just missed the taste of killing."

"There are sixteen Black and Tans wandering the streets of England as we speak who would attest that, like the rest of my comrades in Mayo, I never have had much of a taste for such things."

"They may be difficult to locate, even if we could be arsed to look for your character witnesses."

We were quiet again for a minute and we stared at each other across Hanby's desk.

"You know something, Inspector?" I asked.

"What?"

"I've been thinking as we've been sitting here about a few things, not just politics."

"Fuck it. I have time. Why don't you enlighten me with *your* insights."

My mouth was filling from the bleeding caused by Hanby's blow, so I spat the blood onto his floor. Hanby's face soured in disgust. "Sorry about that," I said, "but you sort of brought that on yourself. I'm hardly in a position to use a scented handkerchief."

Hanby grunted. I suspected he was thinking, "Dirty Fenian bastard."

"Motive, means and opportunity—that is the categorical trinity that proper police look for in a murder enquiry isn't it?" I asked.

"This is what you learned in law school?"

"Aye, and a few other places."

"So what about it?"

"Well, with me you have fuck all of those. Try taking that before a judge and you'll get laughed out of court."

"I've been to court many times, Michael. I have not yet met a judge who has found my police work funny," he said. "You see you seem to be of the impression that the job of the detective is to identify the criminal. I, on the other hand, think the job of the detective, is to find the evidence to convict the suspect. And that is something that I am confident I can do with you."

"How? We've already established I did not have much of a motive. I'm sure, given the sort of Hoey, you could easily find half a dozen men with a better motive than me. Maybe Anthony had an uncle or two who know a bit about killing and did decide to avenge the young fella. Maybe there is somebody who took a different point of view than Hoey on the Treaty and decided to even a different score."

"Maybe. But why should I bother my arse looking for any of them when I already have you?"

"I don't even have a gun. I did not have the opportunity."

"Michael, this station is full of guns. Do you think I will have any difficulty finding one for you? And as for opportunity, as you said yourself, you live in close proximity to Hoey. So you could have had all sorts of opportunities, couldn't you? All Europe was convulsed with slaughter just because Archduke Ferdinand's driver took a wrong turn past the shop where Gavrilo Princip was having a sandwich. Maybe Hoey just took a different wrong turn and bumped into you munching a proverbial ham bap."

"For that to have happened I would have to have been tooled up at all times. What sort of an eejit would I be to be wandering the countryside with a revolver in my belt? South Armagh is hardly Sarajevo let alone Santa Fe, and your goons would have a field day with me if I was ever caught in possession."

Hanby was silent for a while. Then he sighed. "You know Michael you might have made a decent lawyer if you had not decided upon a career of lawlessness. But you will have plenty of time to reflect upon that in jail. Because I'll tell you what is going to happen now. I am going to write out your confession to the murder of Cathal Hoey and it will be typed up. And then some time over the coming days, you are going to sign that confession."

"I am in my fuck."

"No, Michael you are. That's just the way it is. You know it, and I know it. Like you said, I really don't want a judge having chuckle at my expense when we go to court."

"But I didn't kill Hoey," I said.

"So you keep saying, Michael. But haven't you grasped the futility of that yet? I have, as you have already noted, a team of very dedicated constables in this station. Already they are being organised into teams so that we can provide you with the constant care and attention necessary for you to see the importance of complying with our simple request: that you, for the good of your own soul and of the wider community at large, confess to what you did."

Hanby pressed the buzzer on his desk. After a moment I heard a distant tramp of boots coming towards us. "On the bright side," said Hanby, "I'm a slow writer. So you will have an hour or so to come to your senses before things have to get nasty."

The footsteps got louder and there was a knock at the office door. "Enter," Hanby shouted. Two big, uniformed peelers came in. "Take Mr McAlinden down to the holding cells. I'm giving him a couple of hours to reflect on what he has done. Then we'll be speaking to him again."

XXVI

They delivered me to my cell with just a single boot up the hole to remind me of what would await if I didn't sign the confession when they returned. Then they left me to stew.

It was a different cell from the one I had been in previously, but just as cold. But I didn't feel the cold, just the fear of what was coming. I paced the cell until I was dizzy and then tried to sit. But I couldn't sit and started to pace again.

I had no watch, so the only thing marking the passage of time was the shifting light through the narrow window of the cell. I reckoned I must have been there about three hours before I heard the tramp of the boots to take me for my first kicking. How many of these would there be before I finally signed? I knew at some point I would certainly crumble, but I had to resist.

The door opened and I turned to face the wall, preparing to be handcuffed again. "No," said one of the peelers. "This way!"

The two peelers led me out of the cell and escorted me up a set of stairs. But rather than the direction of Hanby's office they guided me along a different route. Of course, I realised, for a serious beating they would not do it in an inspector's office, for fear of all the blood. Rather I was being brought somewhere that would be easier to sluice out.

But that, it transpired, wasn't the plan either. Instead I found myself in the foyer of the station. A burly sergeant behind the desk handed me a cardboard box with my belt, boots and other personal effects inside.

"Sign here," he said, pointing to a receipt on the barrack's counter. I did as he asked. It was already dated. "Now don't come back here if you know what is good for you," he said, and once more I was bundled out onto the street.

It was empty of both cars and pedestrians. I wondered for a moment if I was in a dream but, as I stumbled over a stone in my stockinged feet, I realised that I was indeed wide awake.

If this was some catastrophic bureaucratic mistake on their part I thought it was probably a good idea to get as far away from the barracks as possible. I walked fast around the corner and didn't pause to put my boots on until I had turned into yet another street.

Sitting on the kerb, I could feel my heart pounding so I tried to calm myself with deep breaths. I shuffled through the rest of my possessions in the box. I took out the belt and re-threaded it into my trousers and fastened my watch around my wrist. The last item was my wallet. I checked it and the ten-bob note that was meant to last me to my next payday was still there.

I looked around and there was a pub on the corner. I pushed myself to my feet and made my way unsteadily to the door.

Inside, there were half a dozen old men scattered around the bar. Their pipe smoke hung like incense in the golden evening light. It was not a pub that I was familiar with, but I knew how they worked. I pulled up a stool and sat down at the bar. The publican, a middle-aged man with a friendly smile, came up to me. "What can I get you?" he asked.

"A pint and a whiskey," I said, "and a pint glass of water too, please."

XXVII

I could have stayed in that pub drinking for as long as my money lasted. But once I'd finished my porter and whiskey I headed back outside. A bit lighted headed with the drink I made my way back towards the abattoir where I found my bike, still safely locked up. How long were they going to let me keep this job if I kept getting dragged out by the peelers, missing work and causing all manner of disruption in the workplace.

There was time to worry about that latter. For now I mounted my bike and headed for the Dublin Road. But I didn't go home. Instead, I made my way to the married sister's house in Meigh.

She was a Rodgers now, so maybe not such an obvious connection with the rest of the family. Her husband, Tomás, was, like herself, a national school teacher and they were married coming up to four years now, with one son, Michael, born when I was in prison, but, my sister told me, named after our maternal grandfather in case I was 'getting notions'.

I had only met Tomás for the first time a few months ago, after I got out of jail. But he couldn't have been nicer to me this evening. He gave me some of his own clean clothes so I could change and a lend of his razor so I could wash and shave.

Once Tomás had seen me settled in the kitchen with another glass of whiskey and a bowl of stew he mounted up on his own bicycle to bring news to the parents in Killean that I was out of jail and safe, and would be staying with him and Ursula for a few days until we saw what way the wind was blowing with the police.

However, no sooner than he was gone, my sister put little Michael out into the back garden to play for a bit so she could have the necessary privacy to light into me. In an expansive tirade that ranged across every bad decision I had ever made in my life, including a variety of offences that I had committed before I was even into secondary school, Ursula set out the prosecution case for how I had "broken our poor mother's heart."

"You should be ashamed of yourself," she concluded. I think she could have kept going if she didn't have to stop to breathe.

"I am," I said, "even though I haven't actually done anything wrong."

"Maybe not this time," said Ursula.

"What? You are so unimpeachably pure? Our Joe told me about the time that you lost me when you were meant to be taking care of me."

"Well, we found you again."

"Aye! Climbing into the pigsty."

"Well, it did no harm to you, did it?"

"Or that time you went sneaking out to the dance after our Ma told you that you were not allowed to go. Sure we were out half the night hunting for you after you were found out. You couldn't even go gallivanting without causing a commotion."

"That is hardly on a par with you flinging away all the money for your education by you going off gallivanting with the IRA. All the rest of the shite, right down to this latest mess with the peelers, stems from that."

"I was trying to do the right thing."

"Well, God forbid you ever try to do the wrong thing then, when we end up in this much shite from your good intentions."

I took a sip of my whiskey. I had had that thought myself more than once over the past few years, particularly over these past few weeks, about how much evil can be done by the implacable wielding righteousness. Because there was that awkward and inexorable fact, that when you made a mistake with the shooting, or withholding medical treatment, it was not a thing that could ever be undone.

Saturday 20 June 1925

XXVIII

I had received a note from Sophia the day after I was released suggesting we meet again for coffee. She had delivered it that morning to the house in Killean and Joe had brought it over to me at Ursula's house the next evening. "Usual place, usual time," the note had said. So, as usual, I waited for her and she was a bit late.

It was the same waitress from before and she was all smiles and curiosity again when I sat down.

"Still on the *Don Quixote*," she asked.

"Aye," I said. "I think I will be another week or so with this."

"I usually speed through the books that I like."

"I do like this," I said, "but I've had a few interruptions these past couple of weeks."

"Well, have you worked out what it is about yet?"

"I'm still not sure. I think it's a bit like Shakespeare: different readers, different audiences can take different things from it, and each rereading, each new performance might yield up something new."

"But what about this reading for you?"

"I'm still thinking about it, but one thing I think it is definitely about is the importance of your friends getting you through shite times in your life, even if you and they are eejits."

"It's about all of human life then?"

"That's definitely one way of putting it."

"Are you meeting your friend again today."

"Aye, I've been doing a bit of work for her."

"What sort of work?"

"Research, I suppose."

"I don't mean to be rude, but you do not look much like a researcher."

I laughed. "I suppose not. I used to study law. Now I'm a poor student fallen on hard times."

"Ah, God love you. Where did you study law?"

"Galway."

"Lovely," she said. "We went on our summer holidays to Galway once. But I'm off to Dublin in October."

"What for?"

"To study English."

"Trinity?"

"Not at all. University College Dublin."

"Good for you. Enjoy it. You'll miss it when it is over."

"I plan to. But in the meantime, I'll get you a coffee."

"Actually, do you know what would be lovely instead?"

"Your wish is my command."

"A cup of tea then, if you please."

"My pleasure," she said, and off she went.

I was fifteen minutes reading over my tea before Sophia arrived.

"Sorry I'm late," she said. "I had to go to the shop to pick something up. So, you're on the tea today?" she asked as she settled herself at the table, placing her bags on a spare chair.

"I didn't know how long you would be. I thought it would be better having a tea than be buzzing on coffee by the time you arrived."

"Well, do you want another tea now, or will you be having a coffee."

"I think I will stick with the tea. They make a grand cup here."

Sophia waved to the waitress, who immediately came over.

"Hello again, Aoife. Could I get a coffee please. And you'll have another tea, Mick?"

"I will thanks," I said.

"And another tea for Mick," said Sophia.

"Would you like any cakes or buns?" Aoife asked.

"Not for me thanks," I said.

"Me neither," said Sophia.

"Grand so," said Aoife, and off she went towards the kitchen.

"How did you know her name?" I asked.

"I asked her."

"When?"

"The last time we were in. 'Twas hardly witchcraft," said Sophia.

I took a mouthful of the cold tea that I had left before me. "So how have you been," I asked.

"Surviving. Work keeps me busy. How about you?"

"Well, work keeps me busy too, but it leaves me a lot of time for worrying."

"What is worrying you?" asked Sophia.

"Hanby left me with a very clear understanding that I was going to sign a confession to killing Hoey, or be beaten to a bloody pulp. And then with no explanation I was released. I'm wondering is he playing some 'cat and mouse' shite like the peelers did with the Suffragettes."

"I know what you mean, Mick. But I think we might be out of the woods by now."

"What do you mean 'we'?"

"I told you I had a solicitor? I got a number of recommendations for good lawyers when I first arrived in town. I needed someone to do the conveyancing for my house. Anyway I picked this one, Brian McDonald, because he's also a Labour councillor in town. I had a soft spot for the Labour party in my Dublin days. Anyway, it turns out he's also handled much of the representation for IRA and other political prisoners for much of the past decade."

"Go on."

"Well, there is not much gets past him, with his contacts in the police and the countryside. After you were last lifted I told him to keep an ear out for you, to assume representation for you if ever you were lifted again, and to let me know."

"That's remarkably kind of you, Sophia. But I saw neither hide nor hair of this McDonald fella, before or since I've been inside."

"Well, you wouldn't have. But shortly after you got picked up he got word of it."

"How?"

"That he won't say. I don't know. Maybe a tame cop, or a Catholic cleaner in the station. Anyway he was quick enough to find out why you were lifted and to glean some details of the case."

"So what happened then?"

Sophia smiled but before she could say anything Aoife was back at our table with the fresh drinks which she served to us with her customary dexterity.

"Lovely," said Sophia.

"Many thanks," I said.

We waited until Aoife returned to the kitchen, then Sophia continued. "Mr McDonald came to see me. He knew you were lifted under the Emergency Powers and given what you were lifted for he was pretty sure he was not going to be able to see you until after you had signed a confession."

"So how come I am out."

"I decided to take a chance."

"What sort of chance?"

"I told Mr McDonald that there is no way you could have killed Hoey on the night in question."

"How could you know that?"

"Faith," said Sophia.

That was a word I had not been expecting and it took me aback. "You think I am that good?" I asked.

"If you're not, I'm pretty sure you're that careful."

"I'm afraid none of that is regarded as having a strong evidentiary base, particularly in murder trials."

"I know," said Sophia. "So I told him something more."

"What exactly?"

"I told him that you were with me."

I felt my mouth drop open. "You did what?" I asked.

"I told Mr McDonald that you could not have killed Hoey because you had spent the night with me."

"Fuck," I said.

"I suppose that is another way of putting it."

"Fuck."

"You know there are nicer words. Making love maybe?"

"Fuck."

"Mick, if you are going to fixate upon this bit, then I am not going to have time to tell you the rest."

In silence still, I looked at Sophia and tried to formulate just one sensible question. "So what happened then?" I finally managed.

"I gave Mr McDonald my witness statement."

"Saying that we had spent the night together?"

"Haven't we been over that bit, Mick?"

"But we didn't," I said.

"They are not to know that."

"They are police. It is their job to find out such things."

"I described a situation for which there are just two witnesses: you and me. You arrived at my place just past midnight and left just before dawn. You were on your bicycle so you made no noise arriving, but even on a bicycle, you could not have been anywhere near Hoey's killing."

"I could imagine a prosecuting barrister having a field day with that one."

"How so?"

"For a start I have only ever been to your house once, and then it was only the garage and the kitchen that I saw. Description of the rest of the house would trip me up even before we ever got to anything more intimate."

"It was dark. You were not looking at the fecking wallpaper."

"Okay then. Any birthmarks? Other distinguishing features?"

"No. My skin is like alabaster."

"Jesus."

"Breasts like pomegranates."

"Sophia! You do not seem to be taking this very seriously!"

"Look, we can cross those bridges if ever we come to them. The thing is that it was something for us to go to Hanby with."

"We?"

"Mr McDonald thought that it would be more powerful if I accompanied him on his visit to see the inspector."

"So you wandered in and told Hanby that we had been at it all night and so I couldn't have killed Hoey and hoped he would not probe any further."

"There you go!"

"We're going to jail," I said.

"If that was true, you would still be in the barracks with fewer teeth than you currently have."

"I don't get it. I may not be the greatest detective in the world, but I think even I could pick apart that alibi. Why didn't Hanby?"

"He did ask why, if you had such a rock solid alibi, you hadn't mentioned it to him when he was interrogating you. I pointed out that, as he well knew, you had previous about not breaking professional confidences. So he should hardly be surprised that you wouldn't easily go blabbing about personal ones either. All in all, I think, maybe, he was unsettled by the story: a woman, and a Protestant to boot, being prepared to risk her reputation in open court might prove convincing to a judge no matter how ill disposed towards the IRA the said judge was. More to the point it might draw attention to the evidence, medical and otherwise, of any torture and ill-treatment used to coerce a confession. That was McDonald's argument anyway. To my eyes it certainly gave Hanby pause."

"Fuck."

"Yes, Mick. We've been over that bit."

"I'm more scared now than I was when I sat down at this table. I'm scared for you now."

"I'm scared for me too. But really, I got you into this mess. I thought I'd better do something to get you out of it."

"So you just gritted your teeth and got on with it?"

"I did."

"No fucking about, so to speak."

"Time was, rather, of the essence."

"This is too much though."

"It might be, if you turn out to be a wastrel. But I don't think that is you. You've been through the wars, Mick, but there is some fight left in you still."

I leaned back in my chair and sipped some tea. "I think I really need a whiskey."

"I know what you mean," said Sophia. She took a mouthful of her coffee and lit a cigarette.

"Give me one of them things," I said. She passed the cigarette package to me and a silver vesta case. I fumbled a fag out of the pack and lit up. As I inhaled the smoke, I finally felt my nerves subside slightly.

Outside was the normal chatter of market day, people going about their lives with no thought of the anguish at this table. How do you get to have not a care in the world?

"There is something I think I should tell you," I said, taking another drag.

"What is that?"

"You may not like it, but I think there is good and bad to it."

"Go on."

"I think Hanby may have killed Hoey. Well... Hanby and some of his men."

"Jesus," she said. "Why do you think that?"

"I've been reflecting on it. When he was interrogating me this last time he told me that his parents had been killed, and he had been wounded, at Altnaveigh. He believed that Hoey was the commander on the ground at that action. So in terms of motive, he had a strong one. As for means, Hanby has a barracks full of weapons and gorillas who would do whatever he asked of them." I took a sip of my tea.

"That brings us to opportunity," I said. "The previous time Hanby had interrogated me, he told me that you had mentioned to him where Hoey lived. It was a piece of information he did not have before."

"Jesus," said Sophia.

"I know," I said. "I think you might have helped give Hanby the opportunity to vent some of his fury."

"But this is all supposition."

"It is," I said, "but it's where I would look if I was a proper detective. I have to confess that I thought about how I would do Hoey if I was going to—it's an old habit and a bad one. I'm trying to quit. But Eamon was right. It really is more than a one man job if you don't want to leave it to chance and you do want to get away with it." I took a last drag on my cigarette and then stubbed it out. The occasional one for medicinal purposes might be okay, but I did not want to be starting this habit again.

"There is one other thing," I said. "I bumped into a police roadblock last weekend. It was at a sort of unusual place, on a side road rather than the main Dublin Road. Peelers tend not to like such set ups: they get less traffic and run greater risks. I didn't think much about it at the time, but now I think that it wasn't about either intelligence gathering or just hassling people going about their daily business. I think it was a screening for a surveillance operation, one that was to prepare for an assassination."

I drank some more of my tea. "I don't know precisely how they would have done it. Maybe they laid in wait and lifted him as he wandered round his out-houses at night. Or maybe they picked him up on his way home from a pub? He was a big man, but they have big peelers too, and with a bit of organisation they could have lifted him quietly enough. The blow of a truncheon could always be obscured with a carefully placed gunshot. Whatever way they did it, once they nabbed him it was just a matter of moving him into Northern Ireland

and putting two into him. They had control of the investigation then so they can just declare it the handiwork of some random gunman, and then pick whatever poor eejit took their fancy to carry the can. Two birds with one stone, like. It must have appealed to Hanby's Protestant sense of thrift."

Sophia was silent as she took all this in. "But wouldn't such a thing risk an international incident if it ever got out?" she asked.

"I don't think it would be in either government's interest for that to happen. Both states are trying to stabilise themselves now, get onto something that passes for a more civilised footing. Anyway, Hoey was anti-Treaty, so he would not have that many friends in the Free State government these days. It's not like they are going to weep too many tears over the fucker even if they were prepared to risk the unpleasantness with such an accusation against the Northern state, which they wouldn't be. That would reek too heavily of specks and logs."

"What do you mean?"

"I mean that before Michael Collins's death, while Chairman of the Provisional Government of the Free State, he was waging wholesale war on Northern Ireland."

"He was what?"

"Well, from what I heard from the Northern Volunteers when I was in prison, he was the driving force behind the 1922 offensive in the North. And he was the one who gave the order for Reggie Dunne and Joe O'Sullivan to kill Henry Wilson in London. I think he had a skinful of that old bigot's encouragement of pogroms in the North."

"Well, that turned out well, didn't it? We now have such a utopian ideal of religious harmony."

"I'm not sure that diplomatic words, or violent deeds could ever have changed much about the Northern Ireland government's attitudes towards Catholics. But that was Collins: he loved not wisely but too well."

"I think I would prefer to be loved wisely than be killed by some self-pitying oaf who has become so inured to violence that he thinks it a more reasonable response to a situation than asking a woman what has happened to her hanky."

"Michael Collins wasn't an oaf."

"You were quoting Othello."

"Aha! I see. Well, generally speaking, that is not an unreasonable point. But back in 1922 we were not talking about Othello and lost hankies, but the Northern Government and mass murder."

"And now we are talking about the IRA and mass murder and yet more murder emanating from that. The only thing that has changed, maybe, is that a lot of folks looked at what the Orange murder gangs were doing, decided they hated it, and then did it themselves. Constitutionally nothing has changed. Politically things have become more polarised."

"I know. And I'm sure historians will spend years debating and critiquing the wisdom of Collin's Northern policy. But suffice to say, it provides a strong basis for the Irish national pastime of 'whataboutery'. If anyone in the current Free State government got sniffy about a few cops straying across the border to plug the likes of Hoey then they would be told pretty sharpish, whatabout they go fuck themselves instead."

Sophia sipped some more coffee. "So," she asked, "you think I may have contributed to Hoey's death?"

"Yes... but he was a cunt."

Sophia stifled a shocked laugh.

"I know the thought of contributing to a man's death is a hard thing to carry," I said. "But there are bright sides to this too."

"What like?"

"Well, for starters, it should mean Collette's sister, Mairead, is rather safer."

"I suppose that is true," said Sophia. "Though just as easily she might end up in an institution similar to the one her sister died in."

"That still seems better than the alternative to me."

"Maybe," said Sophia. "But the lesser of two evils is still an evil."

"Sometimes, that is the best we can hope for." I took a mouthful of my tea. "And then from our more selfish perspectives there is this: If Hanby did kill Hoey he would want a dupe who would go quietly to the slaughter, not one with a solicitor and a putative lover providing alibis and making protests on his behalf. Such things might draw attention to the investigating officer's personal involvement and his suspect methods."

Sophia took this in, sipping some of her coffee as she did so. "And all this would have been going through Hanby's mind as we presented him with evidence of our carnal shenanigans."

"Yes," I said.

"If you are right I suppose it shows one thing."

"What's that?" I asked.

"That luck is the residue of hard work."

"Jesus," I said, "you're a calm one."

"It takes as much energy to think as it does to panic. So I try to do the former," and she stubbed out her cigarette.

"Jesus, Sophia. Whatever way this turns out, how can I ever thank you enough for this? For the risks you have taken."

Sophia reached over and gave my hand a squeeze. She then turned to pick her bag up off the chair beside her. "I wanted to lend you a book," she said and retrieved a volume from her bag. "It's only a lend mind. Charlie gave this to me so I'll want it back," and she laid a copy of *Les Liaisons Dangereuses* on the table.

I set down my cup and picked the volume up. "Is this your favourite book?" I asked.

"Not really. But it is an insight into the contempt that the powerful have for the powerless. Know the sort of them, and it gives us a chance to resist them. Oh, and its filthy too. All work and no play, Mick!"

I smiled at that and flicked through the pages. On the fly leaf there was an inscription, "To Sophia, with all my love, Charlie," and it was dated in May 1914, before that 'blood-dimmed tide' overwhelmed all of Europe and took Charlie with it.

"I can't borrow this, Sophia. It's too precious to you."

"Books are for sharing. And it will give us an excuse to meet again."

"You need an excuse?"

She smiled but before she could say anything else Aoife was back at our table. "Can I get you something more?" she asked.

"Not for me, thanks," said Sophia.

"Me neither," I said.

We waited until Aoife had again retreated out of earshot and then Sophia said, "Another thing," and reached into her bag again. This time she pulled out a brown paper package tied up with string, about eight inches long. "Now this is a present. It's a way of me saying thank you for all your help over these past few weeks, and sorry for all the troubles that this has caused you."

"After all you have done," I said, "there is really no need for that."

"There is every need. Now open it up."

I tore off the wrapping paper and there was a black box inside. I opened it to reveal a black and gold Conway-Stewart fountain pen. "I bought you some ink too," Sophia said and set a black bottle on the table. "Mightier than the sword," she said.

"This is too much," I said.

"No, you'll be needing it," said Sophia.

"Needing it how?" I asked.

"Well, I told you all about Mr McDonald. He's tied up with a case for the next week but said he would very much like to meet you to discuss the possibility of an apprenticeship."

"Sophia…"

"I know you wanted to be a barrister. But solicitors maybe have the more urgent job. They are the ones who have to face down the police when they are misbehaving, just like Mr McDonald did for you. A tough nut like yourself would revel in that sort of thing."

"Sophia…"

"Wait," she said. "I also spoke to Sparky."

"Bishop Crosby?"

"The very man. He reckons he may be able to pull a few strings to get you entry to St Joseph's Teacher Training College in Belfast this October if you wanted. There is also some scholarship money available at his discretion."

"Sophia…" I said again.

"The point is you have choices. It's up to you now whether you want to continue at what you are at, or learn how to work with that pen instead, help argue a better society into existence, one that will finally end some of the shite we have seen these past months."

"I don't know what to say."

"Well, don't say anything then. Just drink your tea and chat to your family about it when you get home. You can tell me what you want to do next week. Same time suit you, give or take?"

I nodded. I realised that I probably couldn't speak.

She took a sip from her cup. I noticed that again, like the first time we had met here, her lipstick smeared the rim as she did so.

"My, they do make nice coffee here," she said.

XXIX

When I got home I leaned my bicycle against the gable end wall of our house, and peered through the kitchen window. My mother was there alone. She looked to be making bread or another cake. I tapped the glass. She looked up a little startled. Then she put down the rolling pin she was using and hurried out.

"Mick!" she said, wiping her hands on her apron.

"'Tis," I replied.

"Come here, son, and give me a kiss!"

I did as I was told, and a hug too. She began to sob. "Now, now, Ma. Everything is okay."

"Are you staying?" she asked as her breathing steadied.

"I am. I think our Ursula has had enough of me."

"Are your troubles sorted?"

"I think they might be."

"Thanks be to God," she said. "What happened?"

"Where's the Da?"

"He's off to the market with Joe."

"Well, sure I'll tell youse all the news this evening when everyone is back." I still hadn't worked out about what I would tell them about Sophia's fibs. Much as they liked her, I still thought they would be shocked and appalled at her tale of shenanigans and potential perjury. Maybe I could just skip over that bit and focus on Mr McDonald's brilliant lawyering.

I could tell my mother was a bit frustrated with my reticence, but she had learned endurance with me. She had had to. So instead she asked, "Will I put the kettle on?"

"Aye. In about an hour. I just need to do a couple of things in the barn. I think there is a nut or something loose on my bike. I'll be in once I've sorted myself out."

I retrieved my bicycle and wheeled it into the barn. I gave it a few minutes until I heard the door of the house closing, signalling that my mother had returned to her baking. Then I walked across the yard to the tool shed and took out a spade.

I climbed the steps up to the vegetable garden that the Da kept behind the house and, once there, I paced my way carefully along the back wall of the garden, to a spot that I had chosen three years ago, when I first came home from Mayo.

I planted the blade of the spade at the edge of a loose flagstone. It came up easy. Then in the soft earth beneath it I began to dig. After a few minutes I hit a box about two feet down which I levered out with the spade. I kicked earth back into the hole and replaced the flagstone. Then I tucked the box under my arm and, spade in my other hand, walked back down into the barn.

The interior was bright with the afternoon light. But I set the box down on a work bench in the darkest corner that allowed me to keep an eye on the doorway. I unwrapped an old oilskin that had been tied around the package. Within that was a biscuit tin that was still pleasingly rust-free. I had given it a thorough rub down, inside and out, with bicycle oil when first I buried it. I pried off the lid.

Inside, alongside the pair of field glasses that I had taken off a dead Tan, wrapped in grease and oil saturated cloths was a police-issue Webley revolver, .38 calibre, glistening black, and thirteen rounds of ammunition.

Out of habit I picked it up, tested its weight and checked the magazine. It was loaded, as I knew it would be—five rounds, and an empty chamber upon which the hammer rested to guard against accidental discharge. I had been trained to reload at the first opportunity after firing a weapon.

Who was it said, "*The hand is completed by the sword*," I wondered. Whoever it was probably had never seen the mess that a revolver like this could make of a human head at close range. Nor had they probably ever empathised with the devastated grief of the bereaved in the days and months afterwards when families bury their dead and learn to live with the loss.

Cathal Hoey was one like that, I thought. He probably did not mourn over the dead, injured and traumatised at Altnaveigh. He would have had few regrets over the death of Anthony McCreevy. As far as Hoey would have been concerned Anthony had committed the most heinous of crimes by offending Hoey's honour, even if Anthony had done nothing more than tell the truth. Hoey had not even mourned, it seemed, the death of his own daughter. Perhaps he found relief from her death. It meant that she was no longer around to remind him, or anyone else, of the sort of man he truly was.

But Hoey's own death had not really righted any wrongs or healed any ills. Violence is like that. Blowing out the brains of one man never changes the minds of the thousands of others who think just like him.

So, as Hoey rotted in his grave, others like him, in government and in ordinary communities, would continue to think they were doing good by paying to maintain places like that home in Castleblayney. All across Ireland, similar institutions would be filled with more girls like Collette, incarcerated and enslaved for no other reason than that they were young and vulnerable and female, and their children, if they survived, intended as nothing but chattels for sale.

North of the border Hanby and his ilk would also continue to make the state in their own image. And, if anyone ever put an end to Hanby's life, it would become another cause, like Altnaveigh itself, that would embitter the legion of hard-faced men behind him, entrenching them deeper in their prejudices, and their belief in the importance of not being 'soft'.

It was like Sophia had understood with her talk of Crusaders: Certainty of being right was the most potent excuse in the world for doing wrong. I was guilty of that myself.

I unloaded the gun, cleaned and oiled it. Then I reloaded it and wrapped it up again, with the bullets but, this time, without the field glasses.

Across the fields out the back of our house, the ground fell away steeply towards Carlingford Lough. It was a no-man's land, grazed by the occasional sheep or goat, but with nothing to do with my family other than proximity. There was a place there that I knew, beneath a rocky outcrop, where I reckoned I could bury this weapon so that no one apart from myself could ever find it.

But the wounds it had helped make, and the wounds that it could never prevent, still gaped across these islands. There were dinner tables and beds that would always have empty places now. Other girls like Collette would never be returning to their school desks to wrestle with Shakespeare or the rules of French grammar. Other mothers would spend afternoons baking bread or gathering washing knowing that their sons would never again be coming home for their tea.

Deep as I could bury this weapon, sometimes it is absence itself that is the hardest thing to hide.

Historical Note

In post-independence Ireland, two sets of religious-run institutions—the Mother and Baby Homes, and the Magdalene Laundries—undertook a variety of functions on behalf of the State. The Mother and Baby Homes provided refuge to women and girls shunned by their families on becoming pregnant. The Magdalene Laundries acted almost as a privately run penal system for women and girls, parallel to the official State system. Unlike the official penal system, many of the inmates of the Magdalene Laundries had no recourse to due process of law and many were not guilty of any crime, but merely of transgressing some social mores.

In 2021 the final report of the Commission of Investigation into Mother and Baby Homes was published. Among other things it notes that "The very high rate of infant mortality (first year of life) in Irish mother and baby homes is probably the most disquieting feature of these institutions... in the years 1945–46, the death rate among infants in mother and baby homes was almost twice that of the national average for 'illegitimate' children. A total of about 9,000 children died in the institutions under investigation—about 15% of all the children who were in the institutions. In the years before 1960 mother and baby homes did not save the lives of 'illegitimate' children; in fact, they appear to have significantly reduced their prospects of survival. The very high mortality rates were known to local and national authorities at the time and were recorded in official publications."

In response to the report in January 2021, The Coalition of Mother And Baby Home Survivors described the report as incomplete, saying that "women were made to scrub floors and stairs and treated as slave labour and were also treated appallingly while in childbirth by denial of doctors, medical equipment and painkilling drugs. It is clear from the report that the mothers and children in the homes suffered gross breaches of their human rights; in fact what occurred was downright criminal."

As well as the routine use of slavery-like practices in these institutions, such as domestic servitude by means of the abuse of the inmates' positions of vulnerability, other survivors describe forced adoptions which amount to the trafficking of children under the guise of adoption.

Starting in 1926 with the League of Nations Convention to Suppress the Slave Trade and Slavery, through the 20th Century such practices were codified and proscribed in international law. But many persisted in the Mother and Baby Homes and the Magdalene Laundries for years after Ireland had ratified the relevant international treaties.

'Untouchability' and the caste system that Eamon and Mick discuss in Bewley's, still persists across all of South Asia, and in the South Asian diaspora. In South Asia it underpins the state-tolerated slavery and other appalling human rights abuses, including the commonplace rape and murder of women and girls, that are perpetrated with impunity against Dalits, other oppressed castes, and tribal people.

In Ireland, it was misogyny that underpinned the abuses of women and girls that occurred in the Mother and Baby Homes, and the Magdalene Laundries. Taken in their totality these two Irish institutions represent systems of state-facilitated, and state-subsidised, slavery.

Ronan McGreevy in his outstanding book, *Great Hatred*, explores the assassination of Henry Wilson and the lives of Reggie Dunne and Joe O'Sullivan, his killers, in considerable and gripping detail. He concludes that Wilson was shot, almost certainly on Michael Collins' orders, for his alleged involvement in the pogroms against the Catholics of the North of Ireland. But McGreevy also concludes that Wilson was probably much less culpable for these than was widely assumed at the time.

At the time of Collins' death in action at Beal na mBlath, County Cork, in 1922, he represented the Northern Ireland constituency of South Armagh in Dáil Éireann, the parliament of the Irish Free State. Elected before the end of the War of Independence and the establishment of the Northern Ireland parliament, he was the last such representative. Whether his 'talk-fight' approach to Northern Ireland would have changed the course of Irish history, or even just the course of the border, is a matter of conjecture now. But his death removed from the Free State government its only serious advocate for Irish unification.

The Boundary Commission had been expected, to transfer to the Free State the large portions of Northern Ireland with nationalist majorities. Rather than risk the tenability of the Northern statelet that such a major loss of territory would entail, the Boundary Commission instead recommended only small adjustments to the border in both directions. Instead of accepting this the Free State government in December 1925 confirmed the border in its original position. As a result, many communities were split between two states. In Jonesborough, for example, partition placed the local Church of Ireland in Northern Ireland and its adjoining graveyard in the Free State.

I first heard of the Altnaveigh massacre from my father who knew one man who had survived, it was said, by hiding under a kitchen table while his family and neighbours were being killed. As is described in the story, the violence was carried out by men of the 4th Northern Division of the Irish Republican Army in the early hours of Saturday 17th June 1922.

The commander of the 4th Northern Division, Frank Aiken, was not present at Altnaveigh when the massacre occurred. He was personally leading an ambush on some of the police who might, more plausibly, have been deemed culpable for the atrocities against the Catholic population that seem to have been the catalyst for the Altnaveigh attack. Prior to this, Aiken's military record was substantially unsullied by atrocity. It seems likely that the pressure and horror of the times led to something of a personal breakdown on Aiken's part resulting in him at least permitting, or more probably ordering, the attack.

Subsequent to the Irish Civil War Aiken led a distinguished political career, including as Ireland's Minister of External Affairs. In this role, amongst other things, he championed the causes of anti-apartheid and nuclear non-proliferation. He is sometimes referred to as the "Father of Irish foreign policy."

On the eve of his retirement from politics in 1973, Aiken approached John Hume to take over his County Louth seat in the Dáil. Hume refused the offer, saying his role was in the North, where eventually, after the spilling of much sweat, he became the Father of the Irish Peace Process. This brought an end to decades of civil war and discrimination in Northern Ireland... at least until crass British government blundering around Brexit undermined fundamental aspects of the settlement.

In later life, Aiken rarely spoke of his military career and, particularly, not of Altnaveigh.